Praise for Jerzy Pilch

"A very gifted writer. . . . The hope of young Polish prose."
—Czesław Miłosz

"A highly original voice."
—*Washington Times*

"Pilch's prose is masterful, and the bulk of *The Mighty Angel* evokes the same numb, floating sensation as a bottle of Żołądkowa Gorzka."
—Becky Ferreira, *L Magazine*

A THOUSAND PEACEFUL CITIES

JERZY PILCH

TRANSLATED FROM
THE POLISH BY
DAVID FRICK

OPEN LETTER
LITERARY TRANSLATIONS FROM THE UNIVERSITY OF ROCHESTER

The quote on pg. 61 is from Adam Mickiewicz, "Ode to Youth," *Poems by
Adam Mickiewicz*, translated by various hands and edited by George Rapall Noyes,
New York, 1944, pg. 70. The quote on pg. 75 is from Thomas Mann, *The Magic Mountain*,
translated by H.T. Lowe-Porter, New York, 1969, pg. 517. The quotes on pgs. 118–119
are based on Juliusz Słowacki, *Kordian*, Act III, Scene 5, translated by Gerard T. Kapolka,
pg. 96. The hymn on pg. 135 is taken from an English translation of Martin Luther's
"Vom Himmel hoch da komm ich her" by Charles Winfred Douglas.

Library of Congress Cataloging-in-Publication Data:

Pilch, Jerzy, 1952-
    [Tysiac spokojnych miast. English]
    A thousand peaceful cities / Jerzy Pilch ; translated from the Polish
by David Frick. — 1st ed.
        p. cm.
    ISBN-13: 978-1-934824-27-6 (pbk. : alk. paper)
    ISBN-10: 1-934824-27-5 (pbk. : alk. paper)
    1. Teenagers—Poland—Fiction. 2. Fathers and sons—Poland—Fiction.
3. Alcoholics—Poland—Fiction. 4. Lutherans—Poland—Fiction. 5. City
and town life—Poland—Fiction. 6. Adolescence—Fiction. 7. Religion and
politics—Poland—Fiction. 8. Communism—Poland—Fiction. 9. Government,
Resistance to—Poland—Fiction. 10. Attempted assassination—Fiction.
11. Poland—Fiction. I. Frick, David A. II. Title.
    PG7175.I49T9713 2010
    891.8'538—dc22
                                    2010012026

Printed on acid-free paper in the United States of America.

Text set in Caslon, a family of serif typefaces based on the designs of
William Caslon (1692–1766).

Design by N. J. Furl

Open Letter is the University of Rochester's nonprofit, literary translation press:
Lattimore Hall 411, Box 270082, Rochester, NY 14627

www.openletterbooks.org

A THOUSAND PEACEFUL CITIES

Chapter I

WHEN FATHER AND MR. TRĄBA DECIDED TO KILL FIRST SECRETARY Władysław Gomułka, we were in the grip of an unending heat wave, the earth was bursting at the seams, and the anguish of my youth was just beginning.

The morphinistes were living in the attic, and there was no way to bring them under control. The stairway creaked; first came the vanguard of the odors, then the odors themselves: cocoa butter and something else that I couldn't identify, but which must have been the odor of morphine and immoderation. Every morning—just like everybody else—they went out to sunbathe. They took along baskets of food, drinks, air mattresses, sunshades, bathing suits. Were they really no different from us terrestrials? Quite the opposite! They were radically different. Everyone else went to the real beach; everyone headed for pure radiance, grassy banks, and the babbling current. But *they* went in the other direction, into the depths of the deepest brush, to the very heart of the drought, right to the fuses of the still inactive machinery of conflagration. In short, everyone else went to the swimming pool or to the banks of the Vistula, but they went to the forests on Buffalo Mountain.

"There's really nothing strange here," Mr. Trąba rubbed his hands venomously, "there's really nothing strange. It's a well known fact that the Prince of Darkness feels A-OK in stuffy copses in the heat of July. It's a well known fact that he is mad about the sulfur hour: twelve noon. A well known fact . . . a well known fact . . . a well known fact."

Mr. Trąba unexpectedly lost the thread of his infallible argument.

"We know irrefutably, Chief," he addressed Father, "we know irrefutably that they associate with the Antichrist, but we don't know the operational details, and that worries us. Of what use to them, by a billion barrels of beer, of what use to them is that Babylonian blanket?"

•

Nobody knew why the morphinistes needed that truly Babylonian blanket, which they lugged along with them, in addition to their swimsuits, baskets, and air mattresses. The wildest expanses of unbridled speculation opened up in our puritanical heads. The blanket was great and luxuriant, like the canopy of a deployed parachute, crimson on one side, gold on the other. Crimson and gold like the outside and inside of a royal mantle, like the shimmering surfaces of two holy rivers traversing an empire, crimson like blood and gold like a suntan. There was no such princely covering in the entire house, to say nothing of the room they had rented in the attic. None of us had ever even seen such licentious bedding.

"No army in the world," Mr. Trąba's voice rose to a desperate pitch, "no army in the world has ever strapped such monstrous plunder to its saddle. Not even the victorious Red Army. By the way, Chief, do you remember how the victorious Red Army grazed in my yard toward the end of the war? Do you remember in what satins, brocades, and cloths of gold they were wrapped?"

"I don't remember," Father said coldly, "I don't remember, because as a soldier of the Wehrmacht I sat in Russky bondage toward the end of the war in Serpukhov, near Moscow."

"Oh, that's right. I always forget, Chief, that you are basically a repatriate. Well, these *krasnoarmeytsy*—by the way, they were an exceptionally cultured detachment; on account of their delicacy, my ward Emilia, God rest her soul, departed this world *intacta*. It's quite a different matter that the poor girl's only chance was the confusion of war or the passage of foreign troops. In peacetime conditions her exterior was a bit too radically conspicuous. To tell the truth, I myself made some effort that she might be granted knowledge of the animal pleasures of touch on this earth. But, as God is my witness, it was impossible to ignore reality to that degree. I suffer because of this, and I reproach myself to this day. Perhaps I should have shown greater generosity, concentrated more, focused on those rare aspects of her corporality that were acceptable . . . May the earth be light upon her. Or rather, may it weigh just as much as he whose weight she was never to feel . . . So, Chief, those *krasnoarmeytsy*, who were grazing in my yard, carried off entire armfuls of down comforters, feather beds, and silk bedspreads from the Presidential Castle, but not even they had such a blanket. What would you say, Chief, to the phrase: 'Not even the victorious Red Army had a blanket like the one the morphinistes have?' What would you say?"

"A good phrase, and worthy of reward," said Father, whose habit it was to reward Mr. Trąba's more artful sentences with a shot of blackthorn vodka, and he approached the sideboard, took out a bottle, and poured a shot of blackthorn vodka. Then he raised the overflowing glass, glanced at the swaying phantoms of the addicts who were caught in the oily drink, and said skeptically: "But will you like it, will you like it, Mr. Trąba?"

"There is no way, Chief, no way to like it," Mr. Trąba's voice broke, melting like an October frost. "After all, you know, Chief, that I don't drink because I like it; rather, I drink in order to intensify existence."

Without a word Father gave Mr. Trąba the glass, and he poured its contents in one lightning-fast draught into his broadly gaping mouth. Not one muscle trembled in his face, neither eye flickered, no sigh of relief or of delight was heard. In making room in his entrails for the blackthorn vodka, Mr. Trąba froze and stood motionless. He became like an object, a vessel, a jug that—although it doesn't see, hear, or feel—desires to be filled.

•

Not even the Red Army had a blanket like the one the morphinistes had. But what use did they have for such a lair in 100-degree heat? Why did they take that blanket to the forests on Buffalo Mountain? Probably in order to make a bed with it in a forest clearing, for it was truly as big and as fecund as a forest clearing. Whom did they cover there in the depths of the backwoods? What canopy bed, and whose, stood there among the spruces and the firs? What terrible entanglements must have taken place under that blanket? Or even on top of it?

Father didn't give any major signs, but his gradually growing irascibility revealed that he too was plagued by these fundamental riddles. Mr. Trąba dropped by more and more frequently. He seemed—inconceivably!—not to care about a reward; he didn't apply himself to the declaiming of phrases; he didn't even attempt to maintain a semblance of disinterest. He gaped without embarrassment. His glance constantly ran up and down the stairs over which the morphinistes carried the blanket that blocked out the entire world. Even Mother, eternally occupied with putting her correspondence with the bishop in order, lifted her head from the postcard-strewn desk and, I have to admit, stared without reproach at those two dazzling witches. Their glances burned red-hot, like undying infernos; their venomously twisted mouths were ready to whisper a curse; their sulfurous skin was ready to explode at any moment.

·

You just wanted one of them to be a blonde, the other a brunette; one short, the other tall; one scrawny, the other massive. You just wanted this sort of fundamental contrast. But no, they were as similar to each other as badly cast actresses: both tall, slender, raw-boned, grey-eyed; both had hair cut short and dyed red in the same fashion; both had skin that was oily to the same degree, but that slight defect was so noticeable in its doubling that it must have given rise to a sort of desperate aggression in their souls.

That summer I was chasing after the angel of my first love, and I didn't really pay much attention to them. I didn't pay attention to much of anything. Still, the mystery of their blanket, unclean like

Sodom and Gomorrah, caught even my attention. One day, I set out to follow them. I penetrated through thickets that were as stuffy as the Sahara. I breathed in the smell of the earth, which was as dry as the moon. The crimson-gold panache disappeared from my sight time and again. I parted the branches. I crept through fir-needle brush that was as hot as chicken-noodle soup. But when I surmised, judging by the traces left and the ruts furrowed out, that *they*, that *everyone*, had gone this way, following the tantalizing trail of the morphinistes, I turned back. Even if everyone hadn't gone that way, without a doubt the decided majority had gone that way, and among that majority—although at the same time decidedly outside their group—was Mr. Trąba.

"I have solved their secret, Chief, but only in the visible, which is to say in a highly inferior, aspect," he said to Father in partial triumph.

·

Mr. Trąba was a diminutive, darkish, and dreadfully skinny man. He was deceptively similar to Bruno Schulz, both in the soft intonation of his voice and in his polite gestures.

"Always, everywhere, and everybody, Chief, everybody took me for a Jew. I never regretted this. On the contrary, I was happy about it. Although we both know that being a Lutheran in Poland means having an even more subtle existence than being a Jew in Poland. There once were Jews in Poland, and now there are none; but once there were no Lutherans, and now there are none of us too."

The spaces of nothingness, white as snow in Mr. Trąba's squat and stumpy silhouette, lent him deadly charisma. That summer his hands shook more and more, his features were becoming sharper and sharper, and the smell of spirits never left him. Mr. Trąba more and more frequently, and with greater and greater desperation, expatiated upon the end of his world.

"The shame of it aside Chief, I think that before the sudden end of your life arrives you must do two things: you must do something for humanity, and you must discover how, in operative terms, those sorceresses live with the Antichrist. And I said to the Lord: 'Lord, give me the strength of the trumpets that swept away Jericho, that I might sweep away this and that,' and I set off in pursuit of them."

Unfortunately, Mr. Trąba's story about his pursuit of the morphinistes was a story without a turning point and without a conclusion. He followed them closely, never losing sight of them even for a moment. He heard their voices, even their breathing. Anyway, they very quickly noticed his presence, and they paid him no attention. Once or twice they looked over their shoulders in his direction, and that was that. They were clearly accustomed to the more or less camouflaged sleuthhounds constantly at their heels. Finally, as was to be expected, they reached a little clearing in the depths of the forest. The morphinistes spread the cover, stripped to their beachwear, and made the crimsongolden blanket into something like a rampart encircling their camp. They lay down, and all around there was absolute silence. An hour passed, maybe two. Mr. Trąba wasn't able to report accurately on the passing of time. Doubtless he dozed for a good while. After all, he hadn't set out on such an expedition empty-handed. Even now, after more than thirty years, as I laboriously attempt to recreate, step by step, all the murderous scenes of those seasons, I see precisely this scene—even though I didn't see it, nor did anyone mention this detail to me—precisely this scene, with infallible clarity. Mr. Trąba hastens through the forest on Buffalo Mountain in his silvery-black suit. The morphinistes lug the huge blanket, look over their shoulders, whisper something to each other, giggle. Mr. Trąba picks up the pace, and yet he stops time and again, draws from his breast pocket a soldier's flask that once upon a time an exceptionally—and just how exceptionally!—cultured detachment of the victorious Red Army had given him. And time and again he takes refreshment, and time and again, with the help of repeated sips of the rectified spirits he had mixed with huckleberry compote, he intensifies the will to pursuit and inquiry in himself. If that is how it was—and that is surely how it was—I can't rule out the possibility that the remainder of Mr. Trąba's account was the report from a narcotic dream, which may have taken him in its embrace in the amicable ferns on the edge of the clearing. And so, for at least two hours, complete silence reigns there, absolute peace. Nothing happens. And yet, when the time is up, and the hour rings, a secret movement among the bed of leaves and needles commences and macabre shadows, the phantoms of forest people, an entire throng, begins to creep out from the backwoods. According to Mr. Trąba they were tramps, social outsiders, fugitives, and refugees, with faces flogged by the wind. Riffraff and savages, fallen intellectuals and incurable alcoholics. There was allegedly even a certain writer who, to cover his tracks, had mixed in with this obscure little band and taken up residence in a primitive hut. There was, as Mr. Trąba feverishly asserted, an incredible psychopath with a hateful glance. There was—Mr. Trąba swore on all that was holy—a Stalinist butcher who was devoid of human feeling, and God knows who else. And that wild crowd of men, prey to untamable desires, was gathered a short distance from where the morphinistes were entrenched in their Babylonian blanket; and they remained quite motionless, and nothing further happened. Granted, the forest hobos cast greedy glances from time to time. New arrivals emerged from the forest, joining their colleagues in the clearing and gaping at the morphinistes' lair. They even bowed awkwardly. But nothing else—no crude remarks or gross propositions, just peace and quiet; although, as Mr. Trąba emphasized, it was a peace and a quiet that was full of a singular tension. And that's how it was until dusk, when the morphinistes, with identically melodious motions, arose from the flames surrounding them, dressed, collected all they needed, and set off on their return trip. Then the forest people also began to melt away. In ones, twos, and threes they disappeared into the thickets. Mr. Trąba also arose from his observational lair (perhaps he awoke from amicable dreams?), refreshed his clothing as best he could, and set off toward home.

·

"But I no longer hurried. I didn't even try to keep them in sight. After all, you, Chief, have proved to me time and again that to see what is visible means to see nothing. But if nothing other than what I saw was going on there, then I, Mr. Trąba, am full of admiration for the modesty and restraint of those virtuous girls. For they surrender themselves to a dissipation that is so wantonly refined that their dissipation borders on the lack of dissipation. They pollute themselves on the brink of asceticism, and that always deserves respect.

"There remains one more thing, Chief, one more, before I take my leave of it forever . . . one more thing to do for it . . . to do for humanity."

9

"I don't like what you're saying, Mr. Trąba," Father put down *The People's Tribune* huffily, "I don't like what you're saying, because pride lurks in the extravagance of the certainty of one's own death. We're all going to die, Mr. Trąba. Why do you wish to make your own death conspicuous and give it the devil knows what sorts of sacred missions?"

"Because I know that it won't be long, Chief. I know, irrefutably, that it won't be long."

"Mr. Trąba, as long as I have known you—and I have known you for twenty-five years—you have guzzled rectified spirits every day. You walk around in rubber boots without socks. You don't put on appropriate underwear in winter. The last time you fired up the stove was to honor the death of Joseph Stalin. You are as healthy as an ox, and you will outlive us all."

"God forbid, Chief, God forbid it be so. Apart from everything else, life itself has become repellent to me. But the thing is, Chief, that I have proof, I have unshakable and irrefutable proof that death is approaching, and it is already near."

"You yourself, Mr. Trąba, by the very fact that you continue to live, refute all signs and proofs of your approaching death. And what good will it do you, Mr. Trąba? Don't you realize what an awkward situation you're letting yourself in for? As far as I'm concerned, go ahead, knock yourself out, but you're also blaspheming in the presence of a minor," and Father nodded in my direction.

•

I was sitting at the table on a wooden bench and staring at an open mathematics notebook. For some time now I had been able to solve every assignment in a flash, and so, out of boredom, I turned, more and more frequently, to noting down the sentences I heard instead of solving algebraic equations. At first I wrote at the speed of sound, that is, equal to the speed of the spoken words. Then I sped up a little, and I wrote faster than the speakers, and I always tried to guess the last, and sometimes even the next-to-last, word in the sentence. This was especially interesting in the case of Mr. Trąba. Stylistically, Mr. Trąba was far more unpredictable than Father. For example, in this case I was certain that the final word of the sentence would be "testament," but I was wrong. Mr. Trąba was enraged to the brink of madness, and at such moments his unpredictability grew.

"Here's the proof, Chief," he shouted spasmodically, "here's the proof." And he produced a cheap little graph-paper notebook from his breast pocket, one of a thousand identical notebooks in which I had recorded a thousand mathematical puzzles, and in which I had recently begun to record the sentences I heard.

"Here's the proof, Chief." Mr. Trąba flattened the sheets and calmed his breathing. "As I approach the end, I have decided to put my experiences in order and to write down my opinions, at least the most radical of them. I also wanted to produce my biography and a memoir about my honorable ancestors, but I abandoned that idea. After all, as you have correctly observed, all my life I was in the clutches of addiction, and I owe all I have attained in life to that addiction. But writing about this presents a problem, and also shame. Not so much shame before future readers of this worthless copybook as before myself. Similarly, I am uncertain whether my Papa, God rest his soul, would wish that it be made public that he too, for his entire life, was caught in the clutches of an addiction—and there is no way not to make this public, since my Papa was occupied with nothing else. And my Mama, God rest her soul, was caught, and both grandparents, although allegedly Grandpapa on Mama's side got caught late in his life. In any event, on account of a certain, so to say, aesthetic monotony, I abandoned the idea of memorializing my honorable forebears. I also left out my autobiography, and I decided to content myself with recording my most radical views. But here, too, I was unsuccessful. I began with an appropriate invocation. I scrutinized it, since something in these few lines ineffably vexed me, troubled me. I analyzed them word for word, and I was horrified . . . And I abandoned it, since I understood that I had such little time left that there was no way I'd be able to fill up even a sixteen-sheet graph-paper notebook . . . Listen, Chief." And Mr. Trąba opened the notebook to the first page, and, in a trembling voice, and with no concern for punctuation, he began to read:

"To the glory of the Lord and all His works, I begin to intone this ominous song. To the glory of the barn swallow on the windowsill; to the glory of Buffalo Mountain on the horizon; to the glory of the morphinistes; to the glory of hair and to the glory of shampoos; to the glory of the ink pot and to the glory of blotting-pads; to the glory of the candle lighting my way; to the glory of the pencil with which I write; and even to Thy glory, my hateful little graph-paper notebook . . ."

Mr. Trąba unexpectedly broke off, looked at Father, and asked, according to the ritual: "So what do you say, Chief?"

"A beautiful apostrophe, and worthy of a fitting reward. But you didn't say much in that fragment, Mr. Trąba. I'd say that you broke your quill sooner than I would have expected."

"I said quite enough. Or rather, quite enough was said *through* me here to make your hair stand on end." In Mr. Trąba's voice I heard the distant hoof beats of evil forces. I felt an icy shiver run down my spine.

"I don't really understand." Father stuck to his trivializing tone.

"Did you note the phrase 'To the glory of the barn swallow on the windowsill?'"

"To the glory of the barn swallow? . . . Well, yes . . . To the glory of the swallow . . . A beautiful phrase, poetic, and worthy of reward." Father glanced in the direction of the sideboard.

"Chief, let's stop rewarding me for formal artifice, especially since it wasn't I who was directing my own hand. Have you ever seen a barn swallow on a windowsill?"

Father stared hard at Mr. Trąba.

"Have you ever seen a swallow on a windowsill? You haven't, because you couldn't have. It isn't the habit of those birds, who, you must admit, move awkwardly when they aren't flying, to alight on windowsills . . . With the exception of my windowsill. Do you understand? Every day, at 4:00 or 5:00 in the morning, I see barn swallows on my windowsill, swarms of barn swallows. They go pit-a-pat, they peck, they flap their wings. Time and again they seem ready to spring to flight, but no, they don't take off. They stay put. There seem to be more and more of them. New ones must be landing there all the time, although I never see them in the air. I only see them on the windowsill, barn swallows on the windowsill, hundreds of swirling barn swallows on the windowsill. Any minute the windowpane will vanish, and they will begin to swarm all over me . . . Do you understand? And do you know what is happening on the balcony? Whoever sees a swallow on his windowsill should demolish his balcony—this is the imperfect piece of Solomonic wisdom I have to offer you, Chief."

Mr. Trąba's trembling hand moved like a chess-piece knight on his horse, or perhaps it moved on the trail of other elusive animals.

"To the glory of the salamander? To the glory of the toad? To the glory of the grasshopper? To the glory of the vulture and the iguana? To the glory of the rat and the swallow?"

Father gulped.

"And what do you do then? Do you run away?"

Mr. Trąba shrugged.

"I employ the simplest method, after which they disappear without a trace. At least for the moment."

He glanced once again at the invocation written in a wobbly hand and at the poetic introduction to a litany of radical views that would never be immortalized, and he shook his head in disapproval.

"That bit about the morphinistes didn't come out right either: 'to the glory of the morphinistes'—a hurried tribute paid to extemporane-ity, although there *is* a strong literary tradition of that type. Do you know, Chief, Charles Baudelaire's poem 'To a Passerby?'"

"I don't," Father muttered.

"Even if you don't know it, I hope that you believe me, that you believe me now, that my brain, pecked to shreds by delirious fowl, is getting ready to meet the Other World."

Father was silent. Mr. Trąba's voice was unexpectedly cheerful.

"I've been thinking a long time, Chief, a long time, and I know more or less what I should do for humanity with my last deed. Except that my knowledge is general, and my deed must be concrete."

"Mr. Trąba, if I were in your place . . ." Father's voice echoed with a gravity and a puffed-up didacticism that I couldn't stand. "If I were in your place, and if I truly knew, let's say, that I would die the day after tomorrow, I would live tomorrow just the same as yesterday. I would eat breakfast, I would seek out the truth between the lines in *The People's Tribune*, I would work in the garden . . ."

"I appreciate the beauty and nobility of the idea of living tomorrow like today or yesterday, but *that* sort of beauty and *that* sort of nobility have nothing to do with me. From birth, Chief, I have lived my life under constant pressure for change. For as long as I can remember, I have promised myself that tomorrow would be different from yesterday, next week different from the past. For as long as I can remember, my today is always supposed to be a caesura between the old and the new life. For as long as I can remember, I've been trying, every day, to change something. And now, when an unavoidable change is approaching, when my presence will quickly change into my absence, I intend to do something for the world as long as I'm still here, something which—I won't hide the fact—will relieve the monotony of the final act of my existence on this vale of tears, with respect to both form and content."

"What exactly will you do, Mr. Trąba?"

"Well, what *can* you do, when nothing is to be done, when it's clear that I won't build a house, I won't establish a family, I won't raise a child, I won't put my opinions in order and write them down, I won't render the proper respect to my forebears, and I won't even give up my addictions? What can you do, when a terrible lack, a void, a road drowning in Asiatic grasses, a precipitous bank, nothingness, and nausea suddenly declare themselves? What remains, when nothing remains? . . . Kill somebody—that remains."

Father impatiently shrugged it off.

"A pathetic joke, Mr. Trąba, and if it isn't a joke, then you really must be suffering significant losses in the lateral occipital lobes."

But Mr. Trąba had plunged wholeheartedly into the inexorable logic of his own deduction.

"Kill somebody—that remains. Kill somebody, whose killing will be for the good of mankind. Who? Obviously one of the great tyrants of mankind. As of today, the situation with the great tyrants of mankind looks as follows: Adolf Hitler—*passé*, Joseph Stalin—*passé*. Who remains? There remains, irrefutably, Chairman Mao Tse-tung."

Father exploded in artificial, affected, overly ecstatic laughter.

"I hope, Chief, that your laughter is not derisive laughter, but rather the laughter of a person enchanted . . . no, the laughter of the demiurge enchanted with his own deed, the laughter of God. After all, everybody is different, but you of all people, Chief, will appreciate the dark beauty of the idea of killing Chairman Mao Tse-tung. Weren't you debased by Moscow? Yes, or no? You were debased," Mr. Trąba answered his own question, "you were irrevocably debased in the morals department. And since morality has gone by the board irrevocably, let's at least go into raptures over the pure beauty of our demise. 'Enough has been given to morality; now comes the turn of Taste and the Fine Arts,' as a certain criminal Englishman said in his disquisition *On Murder Considered as One of the Fine Arts*. Yes, Chief, the murder of Chairman Mao can be fine art, and this is irrefutable reasoning. The expedition to the Middle Kingdom itself will be a source of unparalleled aesthetic experiences. Just consider the hypothetical path of this murderous journey."

Mr. Trąba began to trace the map of the continent in the air, with sure and frequently practiced motions.

"It would be simplest, of course, to travel to Vladivostok by the Transsiberian Railroad. There, in the vicinity of Vladivostok, to cross the Chinese border, retreat a little to Harbin in order to gain the support of the local Polish emigration—mostly I am thinking of dry rations, but also of moral support—and then, from Harbin, like a flash, through rice fields, avoiding Changchun, Mukden, and Anshan, to reach the capital of the Peoples' Republic of China. Without a doubt this would be the most economic variant, at least as far as time is concerned. I am, however, in possession of precise information that, in reaction to flagrant intrusion upon Soviet territory from the Chinese side, the border in the vicinity of Vladivostok is so carefully guarded that a Chinese fly cannot fly over it, a Soviet mouse cannot scurry across it. And so we ought rather first go to Moscow, then from Moscow, by trains and busses, through Kazan, Chelyabinsk, Petropavlovsk, Novokuznetsk, finally to Irkutsk, and further by foot in the direction of the Mongolian border. It will be best, as I have discovered, to cross the Russian-Mongolian border around Kyakhta, and then to proceed from there by horse and cart to Ulan Bator, and then all the way through the steppes, the steppes, to Peking itself."

"Through the steppes to Peking, you say," Father repeated, in venomous simulation of deep thought, "through the steppes to Peking . . . And in Peking? And in Peking—then what?"

"What do you mean 'In Peking—then what?'" said Mr. Trąba, suddenly angry. "You will forgive me, Chief, but sometimes I have

15

to treat you like a small child. What do you mean 'In Peking—then what?' In Peking we will have to take a look around."

"As I understand it, we will have to look around for Chairman Mao. But when we catch sight of him, when the Chairman turns up, when he himself comes into our grasp in some Peking alleyway, then . . ." and Father moved his hand across his throat in the classic gesture.

"We will have to look around," now it was Mr. Trąba's turn for venomous simulation of Stoic calm, "we will have to look around for the road leading to the Palace of the All-Chinese Assembly of the People's Representatives. It is somewhere in the very heart of Peking, between the Eternal City and the Imperial City, right in the vicinity of the Forbidden City."

"Yes, and then what? We reach the Palace of the All-Chinese Assembly of the People's Representatives, and then what?" Father said ostentatiously, with the tone of the cynical psychiatrist conversing with his agitated patient.

"Then we find out whether the Chairman is inside, and if he is in a nearby teashop, we wait for nightfall. Mao, like the majority of despots, leads a nocturnal life, which means that it is more difficult to catch him sleeping, since he sleeps during the day. And besides, as you know, Chief, there's no honor in killing a sleeping man."

•

"Oh, I've seen this scene, Chief, perhaps a thousand, perhaps even two thousand times. I've seen it in my delirious dreams, and I've seen it in my hungover waking. I've seen it in malignant fever and in unimpaired consciousness. The swallows, the barn swallows gathered and carried in their beaks a giant screen on which I saw myself—how I deceive the guards, how in the deepest Peking night I suddenly find myself in the Palace of the All-Chinese Assembly of the People's Representatives, an edifice carpeted with unbelievable rugs. I look into the successive offices furnished with Far Eastern ostentation. Nowhere is there a living soul, although you can hear the tapping of a typewriter. Behind one of the successive doors I see the astonished face of a Chinese secretary or guard, perhaps it's even Mao's concubine. She's wearing a dark skirt, a white blouse, and a red scarf carelessly tied at her neck. That nonchalant carelessness testifies clearly to the intimacy that must connect her with the Chairman, who—I smell this with the unfailing nose of the hunter of despots—who is now near. He is behind the doors that are covered with scales of cracked varnish. I press the brass handle. I enter a cave filled with the murmur of his dragon breath. An identical secretary, guard, concubine, in an identical blouse and skirt, with an identical scarf carelessly wrapped around her neck. She is handing him a crystal chalice filled with, I don't know, perhaps it's just milk. Mao, dressed in a white bathrobe, is sitting on a low stool upholstered with a special satin. In both hands he holds the scroll of an ancient Chinese papyrus. He raises his head in the direction of the servant woman bending over him, and he notices me, the black-winged angel of execution, and immediately, in the twinkling of an eye, he understands the entire situation. He knows that I, Mr. Trąba, am a delegate who has come to the Forbidden City in order, in the name of humanity, to do what must be done. And that massive, fat, seventy-year-old Chinese rushes with a hideous squeal into panicked flight. I chase him, I fly after him, I take flight with the lightness that occurs in rare dreams. The white flaps of his bathrobe flutter. His inhuman and inarticulate squeal, inarticulate even in Chinese, guides me. We fly through one corridor, a second, a third. Behind me I hear the patter of pumps on flat heels. Secretaries, guards, and concubines hurry to his aid. I come nearer and nearer. He looks back at me. In his slanted eyes, always full of lavish Bolshevik arrogance, I see black despair, and in normal human terms, simply in normal human terms, I feel sorry for him.

"'Comrade Mao!'" I call as gently as I can. "'Comrade Chairman Mao, surrender, I beg you, comrade. Any further resistance is pointless. Stop, comrade, and surrender yourself peacefully into my hands. You have no other choice, Comrade Mao. I won't give up, I won't surrender, and I won't renounce the execution of the assignment entrusted to me by mankind. Anyway, just consider, comrade, the forces and means that have been invested in your execution. After all, I alone, simple Mr. Trąba, have crossed all of Asia on my own two feet. I crossed borders illegally, I avoided patrols, I swam across the Volga, the Irtysh, the Yenisey, the Lena, the Amur, and the Huang

Ho. At great risk, comrade Mao, at great risk have I made my way to you . . .'

"And in mid-flight, as if hearing and understanding my appeal, Mao slows down and stops. I slow down too. I approach him at a normal gait. Although terribly out of breath, I wish to say something conciliatory before I destroy him.

"'The idea of universal happiness in Communism has perhaps a certain beauty as a literary notion, but brought to life it leads to crime and murder'—I am about to utter that hackneyed and ultimately false sentence. What beautiful idea are we talking about here? The idea itself was crime and murder. Guided, however, by the ritual gallantry that the executioner must maintain toward his victim, I am reconciled to the lie. Let it be a lie, if it will somehow sweeten his last moments. And with this argument I overcome the moral resistance I harbor for lies. I open my mouth, and I place my hand in conciliatory fashion on his shoulder, when suddenly he turns to face me with violent speed. He distorts his features in a hideous grimace. In a flash he thrusts a long tongue, pointy as the spear of a Ming dynasty warrior, out of his mouth, and he begins to scour the air with this tongue, which is coated with layers of green mold. The tongue of Chairman Mao writhes and creeps as if leading its own reptilian life. It writhes and creeps, and patently makes obscene and filthy gestures in my direction. 'Down with Communism,' I scream hoarsely. He produces yet another squeal, but this time an especially triumphant one, and he rushes to the next stage of flight. He flees to a dangerous distance. Once again, off I go; off I go on the track of that squeal. We fly through numerous corridors, deeper and deeper. Out of the corner of my eye I see pictures hanging on the walls, painted by ancient emperors depicting the garden of universal happiness. The flaps of the white bathrobe flutter and are clearly in the Chairman's way, for he attempts on the run to throw off the garment that is hindering his movements. One sleeve, another, Mao slips off the snow-white vestment and throws it at me, but this missile of wadded silk presents no obstacle. On I rush through the more and more intricate labyrinths of the Palace of the All-Chinese Assembly of the People's Representatives, while Chairman Mao flees before me, naked as a Turkish saint. Inevitably, we head toward the library in the subterranean vaults. Shelves appear on the walls; they're filled with the yellowish papyri. Naked and hairless, with the lack of respect for tradition that is characteristic of revolutionaries, Mao makes a weapon out of these rolls, which are in fact reminiscent of huge sticks of dynamite. Time and again ancient Chinese epics, novels, treatises, and dynastic histories fly past me. As Mao Tse-tung throws them, they unroll in mid-air and glide at me like parchment dragons. Sharp papyri, hard as sheet metal, fill the corridor. The tide of classical manuscripts gradually rises. First it reaches my knees, then my waist. My movements become slower and slower, and my sight drowsier and drowsier, but this is the end now, the end of the adventures, the end of the labyrinth, and the end of Chairman Mao. I finally run him to ground in a bend in the corridor, in a small room that may be an abandoned guardroom, or perhaps an inoperative telephone exchange. I run him to ground. I see the sandy, Asiatic sweat on his shoulders. I run him to ground. I stick out my hands, and with my bare hands, with my bare hands, Chief, with my bare hands . . ." Mr. Trąba burst into sobs and awoke from his narrative trance.

This time I had guessed it. From the beginning I knew that the last word in Mr. Trąba's monologue would be the word "hands."

Chapter II

THIS TIME I HAD GUESSED IT. FROM THE BEGINNING I KNEW THAT the last word in Mr. Trąba's monologue would be the word "hands." I had been divinely certain of it, and yet I didn't feel the usual satisfaction that the world was falling into shape according to my plans, and that the tongues resounding in it said what I wanted them to say. I didn't much care about the satisfaction. I sat in our kitchen, huge as the open heavens, and I waited for evening to fall and for the lights of the Rychter Department Store to be lit.

I didn't much care about the lascivious secrets of the morphinistes, about the dying deeds of Mr. Trąba, or about mathematics. I continued to write, but in the depths of my heart I didn't much care about the sentences I heard, and which I recorded mechanically in shorthand or noted at incredible speed in full graphic beauty.

That summer I was chasing after the angel of my first love, and except for those first transports I didn't much care about anything. Actually, I wasn't chasing the angel of my first love. All the later angels, granted—them I chased. But I didn't so much chase the angel of my first love as attempt to establish any kind of contact with her whatsoever. I was like the village cloud-gazer who dreams of reaching the spheres beyond the stars.

True, the brick galaxy of the Rychter Department Store bordered upon our world, but the angel of my first love lived up high. Her floor was a thousand times further away than the attic of the morphinistes creaking just above our heads. Hounded by my lusts, I stared at the whitish planet of her window. My hands shook. I couldn't keep the pen, with the Redis nib, in my hand. Black-green rivers of radio waves flowed gently through white and deserted centers of towns: Nice, London, Rome, Madrid . . .

WHY—I wrote in huge letters on the back of a piece of bristol board on which a few days ago I had drawn, for practice, the classic configuration of two concentric circles, the relationship of which creates a ring. WHY—I wrote in huge block letters. WHY DON'T YOU—I wrote, hoping that the size and contrast were sufficiently legible. WHY DON'T YOU SMILE?—I added a question mark, monstrous in its psychoanalytical depth. And then I thumbtacked the bristol board to the table. I pushed the table to the window. I turned the radio up to full volume. The black-green storms and deluges in the radio played for all they were worth. At any moment they would explode and reduce the bakelite and tubes of the Pioneer to dust.

But will this be enough? Will this explosion attract her attention? After a few, or perhaps after a dozen or so attempts, after a week, or perhaps after two weeks of strenuous labor—it came to pass. True, the radio didn't turn to dust, nor did it fall to pieces, but even so, the worst came to pass. The angel of my first love appeared in the window and began to stare fixedly at the purely—as I hoped in the depths of my heart—rhetorical question written in giant letters on the bristol board. Jesus Christ, what to do? I found myself in an unusually uncomfortable position. Namely, I had pressed myself flat against the wall at the window, my face right up against the shutter. I was basically safe and invisible. Except that I'd forgotten that a significant part of my head must have been visible! It must have been visible, because it was protruding. It was protruding because, with my left eye (with the corner of my left eye), I was attempting to monitor the situation, and I kept checking to see whether the symphony of bedazzling sounds rising to the heavens would lure her, whether she would look at my window, whether she would look, whether she would notice, and whether she would read the inscription. And there you have it: it lured her, she looked, noticed, and began to read. I was determined not to budge, not to move even half an inch. After all, from that distance, considering the matter strictly and without cosmic poetry, she would still have to be looking in a straight line, and for quite a distance, several dozen yards at least. From that distance the fragment of my head could easily pass for a bulge in the window shutter that had been caused by moisture. Or for some accessory hanging on the wall (to tell the truth, that's what I was, I was an accessory hanging on the wall)— some accessory hanging on the wall, a piece of which protruded. For example, an oval mirror in an oak frame. Why in the world, in this place, I tried to convince her telepathically, why shouldn't there be an oval mirror in an oak frame, a piece of which was protruding, hanging here? After all, it *is* here, it *is* hanging, and it *is* protruding. Or, let's say, a cloth bag for brushes sewn by a thrifty housewife . . . After all, in homes, especially in homes in the provinces, especially in Protestant homes in the provinces, you quite frequently see bags for brushes sewn by thrifty housewives affixed to the walls . . . True, Mother, eternally occupied with the ordering of her correspondence with the bishop, is not an especially thrifty housewife, but ultimately what business is that of yours? . . . And I would have floundered on endlessly in that tried-and-true, and therefore unchallenged, bur- lesque, if I hadn't suddenly understood that something here wasn't right, that this was going on just a little too long. After all, how long can you read the sentence "Why don't you smile?" But apparently the lighting wasn't good, the distance too great, or perhaps some other challenge had come into play. In any case, the angel of my first love wasn't able to process the message, which, to be sure, had reached her, but wasn't understood.

And do you know what that scamp did then? She stopped trying to decipher my communiqué, she raised her head as well as her hand, and she began to wave her unparalleled palm in my direction. For a moment yet I remained frozen in my new incarnations; for a moment I was still a bulge caused by moisture, a fragment of a mirror, a cloth bag, but since the angel of my first love saw—quite simply—me, there remained nothing to do but to return to myself. I closed my eyes. I closed my eyes, and I moved along the wall. I disappeared from her field of vision for good. I turned the radio down. I crawled over to the switch and turned off the light. The welcoming banner "WHY DON'T YOU SMILE?" sank into darkness. On the entire planet life came to a standstill.

·

I sat squatting in the darkness, and I was glad it was all over. Time—I repeated a lesson I had recently heard—time heals all. In a couple of weeks I won't be ashamed of any of this anymore. We had come to the edge point, and we call the edge point of a figure that point in the environment at which points of that figure can be found, as well as points that don't belong to it. The set of edge points of a figure we call its edge—I whispered this to myself, and I breathed a final sigh of relief.

·

A locomotive was climbing an embankment not far away. It stopped every little bit like a tired hiker. The engineer said something to his assistant. Someone was taking the shortest path in the world between our house and the Rychter Department Store. Someone was walking there at the edge of night, whistling, kicking an empty sardine can. Its impacts on the asphalt resounded with incredible smoothness. Someone guided the empty sardine can like Roman Lentner kicking a soccer ball. Someone kicked a can as great as a soccer ball. He was just about to make a shot in the direction of the goal when suddenly a defender emerged out of thin air. They battled without mercy. The racket and din were such that it might have seemed that they were wearing not team jerseys but thin metal armor. First individual whistles, then more and more frequent ones began to resound from the stands. One after another the strangest objects flew from the stands, and they crashed with a bang on the grass, which was hard as asphalt.

I jumped to my feet, turned on the light, and ran to the window. The angel of my first love was raving like a mad woman. She was whistling through her fingers, as she methodically stripped her room of all its objects, throwing them down onto the sidewalk. Sure—the thought flashed through my mind—after all, she must be something like twenty-six or twenty-seven years old, and at that age objects no longer have any significance. The angel of my first love drove me from the lair of my virginal fear with a hailstorm of ashtrays, silverware, mugs, glasses, all sorts of empty packages. The lights came on in every window of the Rychter Department Store. Accidental passersby were transformed into accidental witnesses. From afar you could hear the siren of an approaching ambulance or fire truck.

Now it was I who waved to her. I let it be known that I am here, that I consent to everything. I sent her missives to calm the air. I soothed her fury with the help of a mad alphabet of incoherent gestures. Finally she noticed me, and she stood stock-still. Now I slowly pointed my index finger at myself, and then I reached both hands out in her direction, which was to signify: "I will come to you right away, and I will allow you to make sport of my young and virginal body." But she, to my great amazement, shook her head no, and she turned her unparalleled hand down, in the direction of the display window of the footwear section, which was covered with a green grating. I repeated my gesture. She doesn't understand, I thought—or maybe she just doesn't believe her own dumb luck. But no, she emphatically and definitively pointed in the direction of the massive grill which was guarding a few pairs of miserable Gomułka-era pumps. I raised the wrist of my left hand, and I pointed at the face of my watch, a Soviet Polyot with a calendar. When? Immediately, she responded, making the zero sign. Upstairs you could hear the spasmodic whispers of the morphinistes. Father sought out the truth between the lines of *The People's Tribune*. "Dear and Beloved Reverend Bishop," Mother wrote, but only as a draft version for now. My legs gave way beneath me. The night had in it the childish intensity of ink.

The angel of my first love stood before the footwear section. She was wearing an unbuttoned black sweater that reached down to the middle of her thigh. Under her arm she clasped something that looked like a purse, or a document case, or a teacher's day planner.

"What did you write?" she asked with the greatest impatience. In deathly horror I saw, noticed, and remembered everything. In my madness I was quite simply able to foretell not only the final word of as-yet-unuttered sentences—I was able to perceive all of the entire near future. The black sweater meant nothing more and nothing less than that here before me stood—and spoke to me—a woman in a miniskirt. I didn't believe, nor did I know, that this would ever come to pass. It would be a year before skirts and dresses would be cropped, a year before several hundred million women's legs would see the light of day, a year before the earth would become as graceful as the kneecap of a high-school girl. It would be a year and a few months before Małgosia Snyperek, who ran the church-fair shooting gallery in the center of town, would let the unimaginable whiteness of her thighs and knees shine forth, and from one day to the next she would be transformed from an inconspicuous duckling, accessible to all, into an unattainable goddess of sex. It would be a year before all the Małgosias of the world would unravel a band of more or less thirty centimeters' width from their garments, display to our astounded eyes their divine legs, from foot to thigh, and immediately slip away on those naked legs to an insurmountable distance. It would be a year before women again became unattainable. They would become unattainable in the twinkling of an eye, for, in the twinkling of an eye, this laying bare gives the appearance of unattainability. It would all happen in a year.

But meanwhile, the precursor of this revolution stood before me and spoke:

"What did you write?"

"Why don't you smile?" I managed to stutter.

She remained silent for a moment. She looked at me with the intense inquisitiveness of the innate psychoanalyst, and then she said:

"Because that's how I am. I don't smile, and that's all there is to it. Understand?"

And she smiled mysteriously, took me by the arm, and said:

"Come on, let's go for a walk."

It was strange, and, to tell the truth, neither earlier nor later (especially not later) did I ever meet such a peculiar example of the female body: from up close she looked younger.

•

And it was as it always would be in my life: weakness prevailed, but contrariness also prevailed. I ought to have led her. But it was the

25

other way around. It was she who led me, led me through the park that smelled of alcohol, through the soccer field that was going to weed, along the warm river, there and back again. I knew all those places so well that I had long ago ceased noticing them. Long ago those places had left my head. But now she, a scantily clad vacationer, returned being to that which lacked it. I breathed in the smell of her hair. It smelled of Tatar-hop shampoo. I breathed in that smell, and I distinctly felt the gravel of the park lane under my feet. I felt the touch of her hand, and I saw the dark surface of the playing field, the outline of the rotting goals, rooted together with the black stalks of dill, intertwined with the nets that had not been taken down for years. I listened to her peculiar voice, as if stifled, as if struggling with an incessant giggle, and I breathed in the air coming from the river. I didn't know yet that my situation could be described using classical aphorisms: "You will come to know the lands of childhood, known to you through and through, only at the side of the woman of your life," said the first aphorism. "You won't grow up until your beloved looks at your baby photograph," declared the second piece of wisdom. "The first day of your first love is the last day of your childhood. Until then you didn't exist," went the next truth, unshakable in its arbitrariness. To this day I don't know who the authors of these immortal maxims were. I don't even recall where I read them or where I heard them. Their author could just as well have been King Solomon as Mr. Trąba, a forgotten classic or a chance traveling companion, the author of school texts or a young poet whose verses no one wanted to print. Even today it is a question without significance. But then, more than thirty years ago, when the angel of my first love led me through the very middle of the land of my childhood, it was absolutely without significance. At that time, not only didn't I know who wrote the aphorisms that described my situation, I didn't even know that there *were* any aphorisms that described my situation. At that time, some indistinct creature, the winged reptile of fear and lust, began to move slowly in the depths of my entrails and in the depths of my soul. I was happy then that I didn't have to say anything, since she, the angel of my first love, talked incessantly.

•

"I saw you seven times," she said in a stifled voice that constantly seemed to herald an outburst of heartfelt laughter. "I saw you seven times. Yes, Jerzyk—you man, you—I saw you seven times. You see, I even know your name. But I won't tell you my name. OK, OK, don't get your feelings hurt, don't go away, don't leave me, don't break off so suddenly a romance that has barely begun. OK, I'll tell you my name. But in a moment. The first time, I saw you in front of the *Ruch* kiosk. To tell the truth, I was standing in line just behind you, and your shoulders, shamefully clothed in a white shirt, captivated me. Don't be angry, Jerzyk, but by that white shirt, I recognized that—how should I say this to you so that you won't fly into a rage again—well, by that white shirt, I recognized that you don't spend vacations here; you spend life here. OK, in general, you dress very well, but here and there one could improve this and that. In any case, I, a poor sleeping beauty, lulled to erotic sleep for seven years, living in amatory lethargy for seven years, saw before me a teenage boy with very manly shoulders, and I felt that I was waking up. Well, maybe I shouldn't exaggerate that bit about waking up. In any case, I strained to hear the sound of your voice with great anxiety, Jerzyk. I was afraid that you would speak with the macabre tone of a boy whose voice was changing. I was afraid that I would get over it immediately, but my fears were premature. 'I'd like a copy of *The People's Tribune* and *The Catholic Weekly*,' you said in a calm voice that was low and just as harmoniously shaped as your shoulders.

"The second time I saw you, you were hot on the trail of the two bodies who rent a room in your attic. Oh, Jerzyk, Jerzyk, I don't like those two bodies at all. You mustn't take any interest in them, Jerzyk. Why do you spy on them? Why did you go creeping after them? If you absolutely must, why not just climb the stairs to the second floor, today even—knock, and it shall be opened unto you; ask, and it shall be given unto you. I'm not at all worried about the lawlessness of those two. After all, they aren't all that lawless. For instance, the absurd rumors everyone repeats about the morphine. Come on, come on. Those bodies are too lazy to get morphine. They're too languid to figure out how to use a hypodermic needle. They're not buoyant enough for even morphine to give them wings. Jerzyk, you are wrong," said the angel of my first love, and, with all her strength, she painfully dug her fingers into my shoulder and stopped talking.

Although at first I greeted the sudden silence with relief, I won't attempt to hide the fact that, on the whole and in the long run, it didn't suit me. I was completely under the spell of her frenzied and omniscient narration. Even if I had brought along my saving props—a notebook and pencil—I wouldn't have been able to record a thing, to say nothing of predicting the final word. Besides, none of her words gave the impression of *being* the last. Her mind moved with alarming speed and in all directions. It was faster than sound and at least as fast as light, for just like light it reached everywhere. I listened to her avidly, losing myself in the listening, and then I didn't have the slightest idea what to say, how to interrupt a silence that was becoming more and more troublesome in its profundity.

"I'm sorry," I said, just to be on the safe side.

"No need to tell me you're sorry. I just don't want you to imagine God knows what. Don't imagine that I'm jealous over you, you snot-nosed kid," she said flaring up, but then her voice grew milder, and she began to speak as before, rapidly and with gentle persuasion in her voice. "Jerzyk, it isn't that those are two lascivious bodies—it's that those are two *lazy* bodies. It mustn't be, Jerzyk, that on the threshold of life you chance upon a lazy body, or indeed, horror and perversion, two whole lazy bodies. Look in the mirror, my transgressive boy."

The angel of my first love grasped me by the chin, brought her face to my face, touched my forehead with her forehead, and stared into my eyes with incredible intensity, something between that of a hypnotist and an optometrist.

"In the depths of your green eyes, Jerzyk, you loafer, I can clearly see the land of laziness. I can see golden hills where you will bask. I can see the sofas of your many-houred snoozes. I can see heaps of notebooks you will never cover with writing. I can see the thousand peaceful cities where you will live from day to day, a thousand peaceful white cities of phlegmatic architecture and friendly climate. Torrid heat reigns from early morning. A streetcar, open on both sides, is making its way through green pastures. Oh, how sweet it will be, Jerzyk, to live in the heart of that life that is slowly waking but always nodding off again before the final awakening. Open windows, dark apartments, the somnolent dramas of the residents, an oval table covered with a cloth, the remains of banquets that never end, hammocks, easy chairs, old architecture, a thousand gentle rivers under a thousand old bridges, lazy girls going for walks along grassy shores . . .

"My dear boy, I'm afraid it's already too late. If you have the misfortune to chance upon a lazy body at the very beginning of your youth, you'll be lost for life. Your innate tendency toward laziness will be awakened and set for all time, and you'll spend your entire life searching for the promised land of laziness. You'll pass through a thousand peaceful cities. All your life you'll hunger for lazy arms. You won't live; you'll sleep instead. You'll sleep your entire life away. To live, or to sleep, *that*, of course, is the question. But ultimately, as a believing Protestant you should adhere to Scripture, and in Scripture it is written that everything has its time, there's a time to live and a time to sleep. Don't you understand? Those two bodies sleep constantly. They are just two eternally sleeping sisters who sleep walking, and sleep eating, and sleep standing, and sleep sitting. Can't any of you understand that's why they drag their Babylonian blanket into the depths of the forest? Because they always have to have the saving, magical prop of sleep with them? But suit yourself, Jerzyk.

"The third time I saw you was when, in the company of your Mom, Dad, and your eternally drunken house friend, you were walking to services at your church on a Sunday. I followed you, driven not only by the curiosity of the tourist. I sat in a pew at the back under the bell tower. I like the fact that in your Church you don't have to kneel. But I didn't like the sermon at all. The sermon was absolutely horrifying. I don't wish to offend your religious feelings, but your local father pastor gives the impression of believing much more strongly in the devil than in God. Strictly speaking, he believes in the devil without question; whether he believes in God, however, remains undecided. If I'm not mistaken, Martin Luther had that same problem. Ultimately there's no surprise here: either you make a schism, or you play tiddlywinks.

"The fourth time I saw you in the swimming pool. Jerzyk, you swim badly. You play soccer, however, like a Brazilian. Last week I stood on the road that runs above the playing field, and then I saw you for the fifth time. You dribbled the ball faultlessly. But that time, when you set out from almost the middle of the field, and in a sprint you passed two defenders, you faked out a third, and then, one on one with the goalie, with a crafty feint you laid him flat in one corner of the goal, and with a delicate grazing of your foot you placed the ball in the opposite corner—oh, Jerzyk, that was so beautiful that my hands brought themselves together in applause of their own volition.

"The sixth time—anyway, it's not important where it was; I saw you for a sixth time . . . And the seventh and perhaps thousandth time I saw you in your room, where you peep at me, always in the same infantile pose. A thousand identical poses I count as one pose. You see, Jerzyk, I know everything about you. But don't be afraid that I'm a state functionary who keeps an eavesdropping apparatus under her pillow. Or maybe, do be a little afraid. But now, to make it fair, I'll tell you everything about me. Or rather, there is no question here of any sort of fairness. After all, you haven't told me a thing, since you don't say anything at all, and your silence, to tell the truth, is just as captivating as your shoulders. Men, Jerzyk, shouldn't speak at all before forty, and even after forty—not very much. The infrequent exceptions confirm the rule. You do quite right, Jerzyk, by not speaking very much, by mostly attempting instead to record the sentences you hear. If, in addition, you could succeed in shaking off your inclination for lazy bodies (although I know you won't manage it, you scoundrel), who knows, who knows—perhaps you could become a real man. Come here, we'll rest a bit."

And we sat down on a bench on the river bank. Behind us the lights were burning in the windows of the Sports Center. Our multiplied shadows were laid out upon the water. Time and again a single coin of radiance fell upon her restless knees. It turned out that what she had been squeezing under her arm was neither a purse, nor a document case, nor a teacher's day planner. Although all my cognitive powers remained absolutely dominated by her, nonetheless this amazing bit of information managed to reach me. And so, I watched with the greatest amazement as the angel of my first love placed a small photo album on our contiguous thighs and turned sheet after sheet.

I glanced at photos of people I didn't know with the aversion and disgust that a motionless crowd always arouses. It was as if random passersby suddenly stopped in their tracks, approached, and forced you to contemplate their repulsive randomness. To be sure, her face appeared in this crowd time and again, but every time it was altered, in other hairstyles and in other eras. She began speaking to me again. Her hand moved from photo to photo. She told me the story of her family, episodes from the life of closer and more distant acquaintances. I listened, and I looked attentively, but nothing here settled into a whole.

"Here I am, standing on the balcony. A bad picture, but in the background you can see a little bit of Żoliborz. Trusia lived in this house, my best girlfriend. Her picture is also here somewhere. She's no longer living. What can I say? My grandparents on their way to Biały. They had struck up a friendship with a certain German, but you can't see the German; he must have taken the picture. My father, but I'm not sure where. Look, he seems to be standing in the middle of a huge field with a bottle of beer in his hand. So much time has passed, but I still can't figure out where, when, and by whom this picture of him was taken. He's looking somewhere in the distance. He still had his sight then, poor fellow. He's looking as if he wanted to take in the whole world, the plain and the grass. The entire family and everybody else laughing. This was truly a rarity. No one would ever have thought that that was me, and yet that's me in the very middle. I'm even younger than you in this picture. Here I am during my apprenticeship at Mr. Mentzel's drugstore. You see how beautiful I was, how well that white chiton became me. Aunt and Uncle Fiałkowski with little Tommie on a sleigh. To this day I don't like him. Already as a child he had the eyes of a devil. With mother in the window. Do you know that the same curtain is hanging in my apartment to this day? My brother on vacation. With friends on the Cracow Market Square five minutes before *such* a downpour—I've never been so wet in my life. And this, Jerzyk, is my wedding photo. Just don't be jealous. I had a green dress. Just imagine what went on. My handsome husband in a grey suit. Do you know how much he earns? Her earns a lot. In addition, he's intelligent and good with children. He adores playing chess. I don't love him, and I've probably never loved him. He'll be coming here day after tomorrow, on Sunday. If you know how to play chess, come over and play a game with him. I beg you, Jerzyk. If he doesn't have someone to play chess with, he plays by himself, and I am always afraid something terrible will happen then. Those are my children. That's Jaś, and that's Małgosia, and that's me, Baba Yaga. No, not Yaga. Teresa. I keep my word. I always keep my word, because that's just how I am. Understand? My name is Teresa. Teresa, and that's it. No diminutives, distortions, transpositions, forms of endearment. I hate that. I hate that, because that's just how I am. Understand? Just Teresa. No Terenia, Renia, Tereska, Kareska, no Tessa, Tereńka, Eśka, no Teresiuńka. Teresa. The whole story. Teresa at her high-school graduation. Teresa at the beach. Teresa in a ball gown. That one in the uniform is my husband's boss. There's a full vodka glass in the foreground, of course. You understand, Jerzyk, there is no joking with these gentlemen. They mostly don't smile. Even if you were to tell them a delicious joke about an assassination attempt on the life of the First Secretary, I assure you—they won't laugh. And that is mother and father half a year before their deaths. By the end of their lives they had come to hate each other so much that the one couldn't live without the other, and Dad died six weeks after Mom. And half a year earlier they both had passport photos taken. This appalls me, Jerzyk. A horrible secret lurks here, a terrible mystery."

And indeed, there was something peculiar in the seemingly normal passport photos of two old people. She had smiled at the camera, but it was a smile that was not so much artificial as stamped with some sort of desperate determination. In the widely gaping eyes of the blind man you felt the childish hope that in a moment he would see the flash of the magnesium cutting through the all-encompassing darkness.

"Neither of them ever went out of the house: not for the newspaper, not for bread, not to the neighbors. The fourth floor, without an elevator, on Francesco Nullo Street. Jerzyk, I was their doom. And those are photos made in the shop on Wiejska Street." The angel of my first love spoke now in an entirely different manner. Her previous style of speaking had been a sovereign mastery over me and the world. She was ahead of both me and the world by several steps. She knew everything about us, about me and the world. But now her speaking was a desperate defense against utter capitulation. Now she didn't know, wasn't familiar with the secret. In vain she attempted to unravel the mystery. I, in turn, liberated from the shackles of her narrational domination, slowly began to surmise how her final, though absolutely and in-no-way parting words, would go.

". . . Yes, in the photographer's shop on Wiejska Street. When I first came upon those pictures, about a month after father's funeral, I thought that perhaps someone had taken them at home, that they had set up an appointment by telephone, who knows with whom, with someone at any rate who knows how to make passport photos. But no, no way. Here, look, there is a plush curtain in the background. I checked, I was there. They made it there. They were there. Each of them had six passport photos taken in that place. I won't even mention the fact that this must have been a sizable expenditure for them. They had to dress up. Look, father is in a tie, and mother is in the dress she wore the last time for Małgosia's baptism. They had to go downstairs. She had to lead him, although she herself could barely move. Then they had to reach the corner and go down almost all of Frascati Street, and then a certain bit of Wiejska. How did they do it? And what for? What for? Why did they need those passport photos? Where did they want to go? On what dying trip did they wish to embark? Where did they wish to flee before they died? To America? To Australia? To warmer lands?"

The angel of my first love closed the album and stood up clumsily from the bench, and we set off back home through the park and through the playing field that was overgrown with white Asiatic grass. And when, after a few minutes, we stood again before the display window of the footwear section that was screened by a massive green grate, what ought to have happened didn't happen. The angel of my first love didn't take me by the hand, didn't embrace me, nor did she say: "Come, Jerzyk. Come. I too am basically very, very lazy." I was certain that was just how it would happen, but that is not how it happened. The angel of my first love once again extracted the album from under her arm and once again began to turn over sheet after sheet. At first I thought she wished to investigate the secret she hadn't fully unravelled further, that suddenly some idea had come to her mind, and now she knew on what sort of expedition her infirm and dying parents had wished to embark. But this supposition was false too. My first love with the undiminutizable first name extracted a small scrap of paper from among the sheets of the album, and she handed it to me and said:

"Here's my address, Jerzyk: Warsaw, 20 Francesco Nullo Street, apartment 23. You haven't been to Warsaw yet, but some day you finally will be there, and then you must drop by, you must visit me. I'm giving you this address now because I'm afraid that the day after tomorrow you won't feel like playing chess with my husband. And after that we are leaving. We are leaving, you stay—somebody said that to me, I don't remember who. Farewell, Jerzyk. See you on Francesco Nullo." And she turned her back and disappeared, and I also turned my back and disappeared. I disappeared because, after all, no one saw me. No one saw me put the piece of paper with the address into my pocket and look toward the morphinistes' window. And no one heard the Biblical sentence: knock, and it shall be opened unto you; ask, and it shall be given unto you. Even I myself didn't hear how loudly that immortal verse resounded in me, and I didn't know on what distant false paths it would lead me.

Chapter III

"Why are you so troubled, Mrs. Chief? The Lord promised that He wouldn't send a flood upon the earth again."

Mother didn't pay any attention to Mr. Trąba's unremitting arguments. She threw an oilcloth cape over her shoulders and ran out to the bridge, under which brown waters were gathering. I held her by the hand; the massive planks and stone spans shook beneath our feet. St. John's rains had come crashing down a few days earlier. We glanced up, in the direction of the first bridge by the cemetery, and down, in the direction of the third bridge by the swimming pool. The world was the same in all directions. The swimming pool was missing, as was the cemetery. The waters had no top and no bottom. The waters were everywhere. The house a few hundred meters away rested in the depths, at the bottom of a grey ocean. We returned, conquering the elements. We removed our thoroughly wet cloaks in the entryway. Streams of water flowed from Mother's cape. Mr. Trąba's voice came from behind the door; he was finishing who knows how long a citation: ". . . neither shall all flesh, Chief, be cut off any more by the waters of a flood; neither shall there any more be a flood to destroy the earth . . ."

•

Mr. Trąba was almost always sitting at our huge kitchen table, but when the heavy rains, snow storms, and floods came, his presence became truly permanent.

"The time of natural disasters is your time, Mr. Trąba," Father would say. And indeed, our eternal guest did seem to bestow a peculiar honor upon the elements that locked him beneath our roof and chained him to our table. From morning to evening he would sit on the wide wooden bench. When it came time to sleep, he made himself a pallet there, and, covered with blankets or sheepskins, he lay down to sleep, or rather he slipped away into semi-consciousness and listened to the undying gales with an enigmatic smile.

Mother mechanically combed her wet hair with her fingers, approached the window, and stared at Buffalo Mountain, which was barely visible beyond the wall of rain.

"It's quite another matter, however, that the Lord's promise applies to the entire globe. The Lord God promised our first father that He would never again take the globe, overflowing with iniquity, into His Fatherly hand and submerge it in the abyss, that He wouldn't submerge it even for a day, to say nothing of forty days. Nonetheless, there *have* been lesser deluges, I have to admit, and there still are. And—however objectively we look at the matter—we do live in a valley."

"Of course, of course," said Mother, glancing irritably at Father, "we are at the bottom, at the very bottom."

"What are you talking about, Ewa?" responded Father. "My ancestors didn't build this house, yours did."

"That was all that was missing," Mother unexpectedly erupted in elemental despair, "that was all that was missing—for me to have moved in with my parents-in-law, may the earth rest lightly upon them."

"It was what it was." I heard a sinister note in Father's voice; this was rare for him. "It was what it was, but it was high up."

"High, but at the same time *low*," Mother hissed.

"That's just it, my dears," Mr. Trąba sought to mollify them. "High, but at the same time low. That's just it. Let's not forget about the relativistic character of reality. After all, in our lowland country we are relatively high up, but at the same time, in relation to the same local altitudes, we are low, which still gives us a chance of salvation . . ."

"What chance of salvation? What are you talking about?" Father asked in an unbearably official tone.

"Oh, the chance of salvation, Chief, that when the bell tolls, and the waters rise, we will gather the most necessary things, and we will clamber up Mare Mountain, or Goat Mountain, to say nothing of Buffalo Mountain."

"You, Mr. Trąba," Mother exploded, "you, Mr. Trąba, certainly will not make the ascent. Instead, you will float to Mare Mountain or Goat Mountain. Yes, you will float. In the best case scenario, straddling that unsinkable bench of yours, first you will rise lightly with the level of the water, and then you will reach your goal, rowing with your vodka bottle."

For a moment, all you could hear was the roar of the rain and the din of the river overflowing its bounds.

"I've lost track of time," said Mr. Trąba, looking at his watch nonchalantly. "Time for me to go," he said, and he lifted himself from his spot for the first time in time immemorial.

Mother's face suddenly brightened with a radiance that was full of compassionate pity. She shook her head, not exactly with acceptance, nor with rebuke. And with the tone of the loved-one amusing herself with a wooer who is suffering agonies, fully conscious of her allure, she said:

"You know, Józef, that if you leave now, I will never speak to you again?" And she repeated it, pausing distinctly between every word: "If–you–leave–now–I–will–never–speak–to–you–again."

Beyond the windows a stocky figure, protecting himself with a colorful ladies' umbrella, flitted by. Knocks resounded at the door, and in the doorway stood Commandant Jeremiah, changed beyond recognition—his uniform had been altered by the rain storm into the uniform of some unknown unit. I hoped that his monstrous Bernardine, Bryś the Man-Eater, would slip into the kitchen with him. I hoped just for the sweetness of my own fear, but the Commandant was alone.

"By a billion barrels of beer!" Mr. Trąba roared as if with amicable triumph, but in the final analysis it was *ecstatic* triumph in his voice. "By a billion barrels of beer! An officer, on duty, with a ladies' umbrella in his hand!"

"It's raining, Comrade Trąba," said Commandant Jeremiah with stoic calm. He took off his cap and placed his umbrella in the corner. It looked peculiar indeed in his hands—they were as big as loaves of bread.

"Atmospheric disturbances are no reason for an on-duty officer to outfit himself with such homo accessories!" said Mr. Trąba, continuing to play the strict commander rebuking the insubordination of an inferior. Moreover, Mother's recent tenderness had truly inspired his performance. Unfortunately, and as usual, he played his role alone.

It was obvious that Commandant Jeremiah had no desire to enter into a discussion of the regulatory appropriateness of a ladies' umbrella. He brought up a stool, sat down on it heavily, and, after a good moment, he said:

"I greet you, madame comrade and comrades."

"Cheerio, cheerio," replied Father and Mr. Trąba, one after the other, while Mother, in a carefully studied gesture, raised her head and eyes, turned away from the window, and glanced at the green-tiled kitchen stove.

"You are most welcome, Commandant." (I had only recently realized that Mother, in her ascetic role, was a much greater artist than Mr. Trąba, who didn't shy away from the occasional buffoonery.) "You are most welcome, Commandant. Will you stay for dinner? Of course you'll stay, won't you? I was just about to fry some potato pancakes."

Only my masterfully penetrative and unprejudiced gaze noticed that Mother was not a woman who was concerned exclusively with cooking; rather, she was a captive who, in order to survive, *pretended* to be a woman who was concerned exclusively with cooking.

"Comrades," said Commandant Jeremiah, without a hint of emotion in his voice, "comrades, allow me to get right down to business. I have heard, comrades, that you are preparing to direct a pronouncement against the First Secretary of the Central Committee."

The Commandant stopped for a moment and gestured like a stump orator—indicating his essential approval, although with certain doubts and reservations.

"Very good, comrades, very good. Criticism is always necessary to our Party. Criticism strengthens the power of our Party, cleanses its ranks. But you must—*we* must—remember, comrades, that it must be constructive criticism, that is to say, criticism that is, of course, criticizing, but, generally, approving . . ."

The Commandant began to get tangled up. You could see with the naked eye that he wasn't an expert in dialectical argument, nor did he possess sufficient agitational fervor.

I was curious what polemical phrase Mr. Trąba would employ and how it would be constructed. "Complete approval," I recorded in a flash in my notebook, for, according to my predictions, Mr. Trąba's argument should conclude with precisely this phrase. But Mr. Trąba didn't conclude his oration with the expression "complete approval," nor with any other expression. He didn't conclude his oration because he didn't even begin it. He remained melancholy and silent the entire time.

"I understand, Commandant," Father spoke up unexpectedly, "I understand, Commandant, that news spreads like wild fire, but, as you know, speed is not always accompanied by precision. You see, I'm not certain whether our intentions were properly understood."

"Precisely," said the Commandant, "precisely. Let me explain."

He extracted a small Orbis Travel Agency datebook from the side pocket of his uniform, and he began phlegmatically turning the empty pages, which contained only printed dates, saints' names, and names of the days of the week. He finally reached a place where there were some illegible hieroglyphs and secret ciphers, which only functionaries of the secret services could decode—although I was looking over his shoulder, I couldn't make out a thing. Jeremiah meditated for some time over the secret code, but then he began to mutter, as if to himself, and, slowly measuring out his words, he said:

"Yes sir, this is all correct; a pronouncement directed against Comrade First Secretary, yes sir."

He energetically closed the datebook and covered it with his large hand, as if he wished to smother the fuses that were smoldering there, as if he wished to extinguish the gathering rebellion before it could flare up.

"Comrades," he said distinctly, "I have received a report that you comrades are planning an attempt on the life of Comrade First Secretary Władysław Gomułka."

I no longer remember whether Mother froze in the process of scouring the stovetop, or grating potatoes, or perhaps with a match in her hand over the hearth. Today I see her frozen in a succession of these poses. Father and Mr. Trąba exchanged the all-betraying glance of inept conspirators. In the meantime, I thought it might be worth my while to check out the room in the attic again; the morphinistes had abandoned it, and I wanted to see whether they had by any chance left anything else there, besides a ribbon, a mirror, and a nail file.

"The comrades will excuse me, but since the report seemed to me—how should I put it?—only moderately plausible, I set to work in a roundabout manner. If the comrades do indeed harbor treacherous designs upon the head of state, then please, how to put it, forgive me that I subjected to doubt their, your, so to say, qualifications in this matter, but . . ."

"Gomułka isn't head of state," Mr. Trąba, sounding bored, interrupted Jeremiah.

"Excuse me?"

"I said, Gomułka isn't head of state. Gomułka is only the chief of the Party. The head of state is Zawadzki."

"So is it true after all?" he said almost triumphantly. "So is it true after all? No, no, no," he reigned himself in. "Comrades, we have known each other for a long time. We have drunk an ocean of alcohol together. We have pronounced more than one risky opinion together. I can safely—both doing myself the honor, and telling the truth—I can safely call you comrades my tried-and-true friends, and meanwhile what do I hear? Meanwhile I discover that my tried-and-true friends are making an attempt, are ready to make an attempt, at a crime against majesty . . .

"Please tell me," the Commandant's voice became slightly, though noticeably, more concentrated and icy, "please tell me what, in the name of God the Father, am I supposed to do with this sort of information? Please," the Commandant suddenly pleaded, "please tell me what I am supposed to do? I've come here to see—to see to what extent this matter belongs to the realm of fiction, and to what extent to the realm of reality."

"I wish, I wish very much that my death might belong to the realm of fiction," Mr. Trąba spoke up, "but those, I fear, are highly pious wishes."

"But after all, isn't it finally a question not of your death, but of fatal harm to Comrade Gomułka?"

"Unfortunately, Mr. Commandant," replied Mr. Trąba, "setting all my vanity aside, I must put my own person in the foreground and assure you that, above all, it is a question of me." And Mr. Trąba expounded upon his deathbed ambitions in a few sentences, hiding nothing.

Commandant Jeremiah listened carefully to Mr. Trąba's implacably logical arguments.

"If I understood you correctly, comrade, you expect a quick departure from this world, but in fact, what reason do you have to expect this departure?"

"One general and seven particular reasons," retorted Mr. Trąba, and he began to count on his fingers. "First, cirrhosis of the liver; second, a bursting pancreas; third, severe inefficiency of the kidneys; fourth, a weakening heart; fifth, stomach ulcers; sixth, *delirium tremens*; seventh, and the simplest, choking on my own vomit. These are seven good reasons, not subject to falsification, each of which individually, and all of them together, are identically effective, and all of them," Mr. Trąba raised his index finger decisively in the air, "are already prepared. The seven beasts are already in readiness, seven chimeras already lie waiting to jump. Yes," he bellowed suddenly, "the seven pillars of my death have already been erected!"

"St. John of Damascus divides anger into gall, mania, and fury, and you, Comrade Trąba, you are most clearly in the phase of fury," said Commandant Jeremiah, leaning backwards as if to avoid immediate danger.

"I didn't know they covered St. John of Damascus's typology of anger in Marxism night-school. I approve. I approve, and I congratulate you. I, however—and now I will allow myself a polemical interpolation *ad vocem*—I am not in the phase of fury according to St. John of Damascus; rather, I am in the phase of anger with voice, according to St. Gregory of Nyssa. St. Gregory of Nyssa, as you know perfectly well, divides anger into anger without voice, anger with voice, and anger expressed in voice. One way or another I am—I often find myself—in the pre-delirious phase. Vodka-induced psychosis is already knocking with a finger that's as transparent as a vodka glass; it's already knocking on the brittle walls of my brain."

Mother placed the first portions of potato dough on the stove top. The fire roaring below and the streams of darkness beyond the window transported us beyond climates and beyond seasons. We sat in the circle of light, separated from what was further on, and further on were ice and darkness. The Commandant's uniform steamed slowly. Jeremiah dried and glimmered, like a prodigal deserter returning to the ranks of his home unit.

"And what would you think," he said slowly, "what would you think about stopping and giving it up? . . . About reducing the volumetric reckoning a little. You've already drunk your life's quota."

"Stop drinking?" Mr. Trąba neither quite asked, nor quite asserted, his voice colorless as water. "Stop drinking? Out of the question. Already in '45 I said to myself: 'Perhaps you will die of vodka, Józef Trąba, but if you don't have a drink from time to time, you will certainly die.' But now, after not quite twenty years, that paradoxical supposition has taken on a completed form. You know, Commandant," Mr. Trąba came to life, clearly gathering narrational verve, "a man has only one good reason to stop drinking: namely, when he notices that as a result of drinking he is going stupid. Let me put it another way. A true man can die from drinking, but he doesn't dare go stupid."

"In that case," the Commandant spoke most carefully, "in that case, why do you put your lofty mind at risk, Comrade Trąba?"

"You insult me, Commandant," said Mr. Trąba with dignity. "Just why should a man live in stupidity?"

"And carrying Gomułka off with you, carrying Gomułka off with you to the grave," Jeremiah suddenly got angry, "and carrying First Secretary Gomułka off with you to the grave—this isn't stupidity? This is colossal stupidity! Stupidity that is pointless and historically barren. Stupidity that leads nowhere and is intellectually empty."

"Terror is not the realm of speculation; terror is the realm of shock," Mr. Trąba said gloomily.

"What terror? What terror? What terror?" the Commandant roared with the greatest contempt.

"Maybe our terror is not a great terror," Mr. Trąba flared up, "but it's still terror. Better that than nothing. Better a sparrow in the hand than Mao Tse-tung on the roof. Yes, OK, I intended to do something for humanity, but after all, if I do something for Poland, I will have done it for humanity too. Of course I would prefer a great deed on a global scale. Of course I would prefer, as I explained to you," Mr. Trąba raised his shoulders, "of course I would prefer to tighten my tyrannicidal fingers around the neck of Mao Tse-tung. A person would get to see a little of China in the process. But we don't have the resources for such a long journey," Mr. Trąba sighed regretfully, "and a short trip is out of the question for reasons of ambition. You can't expect me to humiliate myself with quasi-foreign trips around the block of the People's Democracies. Oh no, not that, no. I certainly won't go to Sofia to lie in ambush for Comrade Zhivkov. Nor to East Germany in order to administer justice to Walter Ulbricht. Please don't even try to persuade me."

"And what about Khrushchev?" Mother unexpectedly spoke up, neither asking nor quite proposing, from above an already considerable stack of potato pancakes. "Have you considered Khrushchev?"

"Khrushchev," Mr. Trąba seemed to ignore the absolute astonishment with which Father and Commandant Jeremiah looked at Mother, "Khrushchev may be removed at any moment. It isn't worth the effort. I go to Moscow, which, however you look at it, is also a good hike, and on the spot I discover that changes have just then taken place at the highest level of the CC CPSU, and I'll look like a boob."

"And if, Comrade Trąba," Comrade Jeremiah's voice suddenly became warmer, "and if . . . of course these are absolutely not our methods," he suddenly stipulated in a panic, "and if, and if it could be, we could even, not so much help, that's too strong a word, but, let's say, we could *not know* about certain things, uh, even a passport, any time—and if it could be the Bloody Dictator of Fascist Spain?"

"Caudillo Bahamonde Franco is one of Europe's greatest statesmen," Mr. Trąba said with distinct pity. "I remind you: I wish to do something *for* humanity, not *against* it."

It might have seemed that it was not steam that was departing from the Commandant's drying uniform, rather it was the furies departing from the man himself.

"Never. We will never," he panted heavily, "we will never come to terms, Comrade Trąba. Be my guest—kill, kill whomever you wish. Yes," the Commandant suddenly seemed to discern a deeper meaning in what he was saying, "yes, kill whomever you wish. Kill anybody at all. After all, that too will bring the decline of your life into order. Go out into the street, kill whomever, and you'll see in just what implacably logical scheme of events you'll find yourself. You won't do much for humanity, but you *will* do something for *yourself*. And after all, if you do something for yourself, it's as if you'd also done something for humanity. Don't you agree?"

"What do you do for yourself by killing just anyone?" Father asked in a strangely high voice.

"One's life becomes definitively ordered, especially the disorderly life, and your life, comrade," the Commandant stretched out his hand to Mr. Trąba in what was almost a welcoming gesture, "is an unusually disorderly life. A person kills, becomes a murderer, and by being a murderer he disperses doubts and does away with choices. Being a murderer is the guarantee of a highly stable identity. First, if you should decide to go into hiding, comrade, you'd be a murderer in hiding. Then, if they should arrest you, you'd be an arrested murderer, then a judged one, then a condemned one, and then," the Commandant suddenly stopped, as if he had realized that he was about to say something tactless. He finished in a more peaceful voice, although it still vibrated with rage: "Let's save our breath. Be my guest. Go ahead and kill, comrade, kill whomever you like."

"This is painful, painful to listen to," Mr. Trąba said with a sadness that tore your heart to pieces. "Please, Mr. Commandant, don't make me into the posthumous child of existentialism's precursors. I wouldn't even *consider* killing just anyone. I haven't the least intention of joining that godless philosophical current. I intend to join the murky circle of the great tyrannicides of human history: Peter Pahlen, Gavrilo Princip, François Ravaillac, Jeronimo Caserio, Józef Trąba . . . Not a bad list of names," he said, falling into dreaminess, but he immediately roused himself again.

"And besides, what do you mean by 'whomever?' There aren't any whomevers here. Whom am I supposed to kill? Małgosia Snyperek? Grand Master Swaczyna? Mrs. Rychter? Perhaps I'm supposed to raise my sacrilegious hand against Pastor Potraffke, or Station Master Ujejski? Sexton Messerschmidt? There aren't any 'whomevers' here. There aren't any accidental passersby here. Everybody knows each other here, and knows each other as intimately as, if I may say so, you and I, Commandant . . ."

"In that case, why don't you choose someone by lottery, or even better," an almost genuine note of sudden desperation and readiness to bear the greatest sacrifices sounded in the Commandant's voice, "or even better, why not me? Yes, why don't you kill me?"

"You? Absolutely not."

"Why? Why absolutely not me?" The Commandant was not able to check the reflexive disappointment and almost injured ambition in his voice. "Why absolutely not me?"

"Because I don't intend to acquire the reputation of an anti-Semite in my old age."

"Mr. Trąba . . ." The Commandant's voice suddenly broke. Everything was now clear. It was as clear as day who would remain standing, who was already the victor in this seemingly evenly matched duel. Everything was so unyielding that I didn't even feel like recording the final word, which would be declared any minute. I only formulated it in my thoughts.

"Mr. Trąba, I'm an atheist." The Commandant was as pale as ashes, and drops of oily and icy sweat broke out on his forehead.

"Fine." Mr. Trąba danced around his staggering opponent with the murderous lightness of a triumphant heavyweight boxer. "Fine. Just utter this one phrase without hesitation: 'I'm not a Jew, I'm an atheist.' Say it, toss out this stylistic pearl, and I will answer you, just as the Chief sometimes answers me." Mr. Trąba bowed in Father's direction. "Then I will answer you: 'A beautiful phrase and worthy of reward.'"

Father, like a golem set in motion by a magic spell, stood up from behind the table, went up to the cabinet, and did what he always did: he extracted a bottle and glasses. Mother was carrying a tureen full of potato pancakes in sour cream. Thunder resounded, and black rains came crashing down with redoubled might. Mr. Trąba grew gentle and glanced thankfully to the heavens. Father continued filling glasses with juniper berry vodka in the fever of his robotic motions.

"Basically," Mr. Trąba now continued in a conciliatory and almost amicable tone, "basically, it's not a question of whether you deny it or not, Commandant. Don't be angry, but, putting it in other terms, whether you had denied it or not—this is a trifle. Too many ties, ties of another sort, link us. As you correctly say, we are old friends, and I wouldn't be wrong if I said that a step here, a move there, one gesture and you would join the conspiracy." Mr. Trąba lifted up his hand and, without superfluous words, stilled the Commandant's silent and, to tell the truth, none-too-distinct resistance. "Yes, you would join us, but that's not the issue, nor is it a question of your Jewishness or of your Communism: don't be angry, but, to tell the truth, *those* Jews and *those* Communists were quite different from you, Commandant. It is a question of general, as well as universal, truths. Of what Jews *sensu largo* are up to, and just what Jews they are!"

Mr. Trąba suddenly began to search his pockets, and after a moment he extracted a carefully folded newspaper clipping from his shirt pocket; straightened it out; nailed it to the table, which was covered with sky-blue oilcloth, with his index finger; bent over it; and began to read distinctly: "The world renowned violinist Yehudi Menuhin, during his *tournée* of Israel, paid a visit to Prime Minister Ben Gurion. In the course of an informal conversation, both the artist and the politician stood on their heads, since both practice yoga . . ." Mr. Trąba panted hard, and apoplectic spots covered his face and neck.

"Chief, Commandant, gentlemen. A Christian cannot stand indifferent in the face of such things. Yoga, yes, OK, it can lead to salvation, but among the Mosaic prophets there isn't a peep about yoga." Mr. Trąba fell silent for a moment, and then he suddenly bellowed with a terrifying voice: "Convert them! Evangelize them! Show them the road to salvation!"

"Proselytism," Commandant Jeremiah growled scornfully. "Common proselytism."

"What proselytism, Commandant, what proselytism!" Mr. Trąba said with unexpected calm. "I swear on my nine prewar semesters of theology that there isn't any question of proselytism here. It's a question of the Biblical plan of salvation. If David Ben Gurion, who came fifteen years ago to stand at the head of the state of Israel, now stands on his head, this means one thing: a flaw has arisen in the Biblical plan of salvation, and we Christians, and especially we Lutherans, must hurry to the rescue."

Mother placed the steaming tureen on the table and removed plates, knives, and forks from the cupboard. Sitting next to me, Commandant Jeremiah—in whose breathing, agitated gestures, and nervous huffing and puffing I sensed the firm desire for immediate departure—suddenly capitulated and cheered up. Father raised an empty vodka glass. It looked as if he wished to perform a pantomime entitled "The Flight of the Vodka Glass to the Light," but the Commandant interrupted the performance with an imperial gesture, put the date book, which was still lying on the table before him, away in his pocket, and pointed to the sacred place on the oilcloth where the vessel, already taken down from the heights, but still shot through with spherical radiance, ought to stand. And it came to pass: Father placed the vodka glass before Commandant Jeremiah and filled it.

"If a miracle should happen, if the heavens should open up," Mr. Trąba declaimed, "and if the Lord of Hosts should look upon my downfall and ask: 'What can I do for you, Józef Trąba?' If that should happen, with my certain death as my witness, I would say: 'Lord, raise up my friend Jakub Lełlich from the dead, fashion him back again from the clay into which he has been transformed, breath life into him, and cause that we could at least once more have a chat about the superiority of the Jewish-Lutheran alliance to all other alliances.'"

Mr. Trąba chattered away indefatigably, but neither Mother, nor Father, nor Commandant Jeremiah paid much attention to him. They must have heard this story too, like the majority of his stories, many times over, but the great ideas of the Biblical plan of salvation were reaching my consciousness for the first time.

"It is irrefutable, irrefutable, that the rise of Israel was the fulfillment of the prophecy of Zachariah and other prophecies. The Lord of Hosts foretold two-and-a-half-thousand years ago that he would deliver his people and lead them to Jerusalem. And this came to pass, and it must be so until the very . . . the very conversion itself."

Mr. Trąba broke off for a moment, swallowed a significant piece of potato pancake, which had been amply sopped in sour cream, and continued, with a zeal that proved he had reached the very heart of his argument:

"This will come to pass, but it's not the pagan path of yogists that leads here, rather the path of Jewish orthodoxy. Jews came to Jerusalem not in order to stand on their heads there, but in order to be confirmed in their Judaism. After all, only Jews confirmed in their Judaism can attain salvation. As the Scripture says: 'For an Israelite to become a Christian, he must first eat his fill of his Israelitism.'"

"There isn't anything like that in Scripture," Commandant Jeremiah wiped his mouth with the back of his hand. "Nowhere is it so written."

"Not directly," Mr. Trąba became impatient, "not directly, but it's in the subtext, or rather in innumerable subtexts. Just recall carefully, Commandant, Paul's Epistles to the Romans, Ephesians, not to mention Hebrews. And the prophet Isaiah, chapter eleven, verse twelve, and your namesake, the prophet Jeremiah, touches upon this topic in the sixteenth, and in the twenty-forth, and in the thirty-first chapter. Ezechiel!" shouted Mr. Trąba. "Ezechiel! Above all the prophet Ezechiel and the famous prophecy about the field of bones slowly taking on life!"

"I'll investigate," said Commandant Jeremiah in an unexpectedly police tone. "I'll investigate."

"I assure you that you can believe a person established in his faith and trained in Scripture. Yes," Mr. Trąba suddenly fell into a dreamy mood, "that would be a worthy act, that would be an act worthy of my dying ambitions—the deed of conversion. But unfortunately there is little time, and this is the work of decades at least, and not within the abilities of one lonely Lutheran who's caught in the clutches of addiction. Yes," he repeated in a voice marked by strategic deliberation, "let them come to full bloom, even to the first signs of wilting. Let them people the streets and markets. Let us hear the murmur of conversations and the rustle of gabardines. Let synagogues be erected. Let the Sabbaths, Pesach, the Feast of Tabernacles, and Purim be celebrated."

"*Á propos,*" Commandant Jeremiah interrupted Mr. Trąba's visionary trance, "*á propos* Purim, did you, comrade, recently visit Mrs. Rychter and offer her and her numerous relatives help in preparation for the celebration of Purim?"

"I won't deny it. I tried in my small way to do what I could in

48

order to aid in the realization of God's plans, but they didn't avail themselves of my offer."

"There's nothing strange there. An old German family has absolutely no reason to celebrate Purim. And, by the way, I don't wish to trivialize your motives," said the Commandant, "I don't wish to trivialize, but I must note that, in the course of celebrating Purim, excessive consumption of alcohol is practically a religious obligation."

"You don't wish to trivialize, but you *do* trivialize!" shouted Mr. Trąba. "You *do* trivialize!"

"It's you, Comrade Trąba, who trivializes. You trivialize both the Scripture and God's designs."

"But what's at stake here, what's at stake if not salvation? After all, as the eventual assassin of First Secretary Władysław Gomułka, I have no choice but to concern myself with the question of salvation. Of course, I would prefer not to murder him, and, instead of troubling myself with the question of my own salvation, help someone else to salvation. For example, the Jewish people. They who have been dispersed will be gathered in. They will regain their identity. They will be strengthened in their identity, and they will develop diversely in their Judaism. They will be converted. They will convert to Catholicism. And then, without fail, having become disgusted by Rome, they will convert to our Lutheran faith. What's at stake? What more is at stake here? And I would undertake this deed as my dying act. I would truly do this for humanity. Truly. But, I repeat, it's a question of time. And I don't have time. I need something quick, something quick like the flash of a knife, like the flight of an arrow."

"You know what, Comrade Trąba," Commandant Jeremiah said with a phlegmatic, well-fed voice, "you know what? If you really do intend to convert the Jews to the Lutheran faith, of the two evils it would be better that you whack somebody, comrades."

The Commandant raised his glass.

"Drink up, comrades."

And when the men had inclined their heads, and then raised them up again, the Commandant said with dignity:

"For at least the last hour I have been off duty, but in spite of everything I want you, comrades, to be forewarned. I made a request of Comrade Station Master Ujejski. I made a request that he let me know if you comrades should suddenly wish to buy tickets. For instance, for the night train to Warsaw. I want you to know about this, comrades."

Chapter IV

THE PARCHMENT MAP OF THE SKY SLOWLY TOOK ON LIFE. STREAMS
of deep blue air flowed across it. Golden sand poured from the planets.
Within the large constellations you could hear music. I awoke in the
middle of the night, and in the dark, gropingly, I recorded the word
"occupation" in my notebook—in a moment someone would whisper
it in the depths of the sleeping house.

In those days I was never parted from my pencil and notebook. The
desire, stronger than anything else, to record words and sentences that
had just been uttered, or would be in a moment, directed my every
step, waking and sleeping. I would place the notebook and pencil
on the nightstand, and when the golden-black grandfather clock in
the entryway rang out the most terrible of hours, 2:00 or 3:00 in the
morning, when the Antichrist himself touched my featherbed with
a wet wing, when during every season of the year an infernal silence
reigned, I would reach for notebook and pencil and record the word
or sentence that brought relief. "Occupation," I wrote, but I didn't
feel relief or consolation. Noises unusual for that hour were coming
from the kitchen. Someone was moving a chair. Someone knocked
delicately, probably at the window, since the panes rattled. Someone

said something. Somebody answered. I lit the lamp, and Mr. Trąba's voice became more distinct, as if intensified by the light. To this day I am absolutely certain that, throughout my entire childhood, I was awakened from sleep either by Mr. Trąba's voice or by the sound of the Wittenberg bells in the church tower.

A few minutes before 6:00 in the morning, Sexton Messerschmidt would climb the wooden steps, and in the gray dawn of the fall, in the winter darkness, or with the summer radiance piercing the shutters, the cast-iron caps would begin to move more and more forcefully. In the morning, the sound of the bells was delicate like the slowly rising eyelid of a Lutheran confirmation-class girl. At noon, it possessed the fullness of a fire roaring under Evangelical stovetops. And at twilight, it was mannerly and pliable like the mixed forests on Buffalo Mountain.

•

Sexton Messerschmidt knew how to pull the ropes such that he could achieve all those effects at will—the effect of the eyelid, the fire, and the mixed forest.

"You've got to have it here," he pointed to his palms. "You've got to have the divine spark here. The divine azure spark," he added with an enigmatic smile. "Without the divine spark, azure like a gas flame, no bell will ring."

We would leave our packs in the sacristy. The church smelled of the Sunday clothes of Protestants. Sexton Messerschmidt carefully examined our hands.

"Not a single divine spark, not a trace of ability, to say nothing of talent," he would say with disapproval. "Oh well. Cripples have the right to praise the Lord too. Come unto me. Only the pious, only the most pious, will attain the grace of entry to the tower today. You, Chmiel, you, Sikora, you, Błaszczyk. Today it shall be given unto you. You won't even have to put your hands over your ears, since, anyway . . . you are all deaf as posts."

We followed him up the wooden stairs. Then with all our might we squeezed ropes that were fatter than our arms. The sweltering noon slowly began to smolder.

"Let the littlest bell sing," cried Sexton Messerschmidt at the top of his voice, and he looked ironically upon our pathetic efforts. With seeming nonchalance he grasped the rope we had been straining at so ineffectually. "You gentlemen lack not only artistic talent but also physical strength. You are an absolutely worthless generation. When you grow up you will bring not only the Lutheran Church but also People's Poland to ruin—which, after all, who knows, may be for the better.

"This is how it's done. With your entire being, not just with your hands. We are in a holy place, therefore you gentlemen will magnanimously forgive me if I don't suggest just what you can do for yourselves with nothing but your hands. In the profession—in the *vocation*—of the bell-ringer the hand is not an upper extremity but the extension of the soul. Let the littlest bell sing," cried Sexton Messerschmidt, and at his call the littlest bell moved. "Tym's bell-foundry in Warsaw," Messerschmidt outshouted the first heartbeats, "Tym's bell-foundry in Warsaw, bronze practically *in statu crudi*, bronze without alloy, which is why it has a pure sound, even if it doesn't carry. As the story goes, this bell was cast by order of the enlightened protector of the Reformation, Mikołaj Radziwiłł the Black. It was hung by our Calvinist brethren in the church tower in Kiejdany. It served them faithfully, and with its pure voice it sustained them in the faith, which, although perfect, is after all also the correct one. Henryk Sienkiewicz mentions the church in Kiejdany in his *Trilogy*. Unfortunately, Sienkiewicz's pen did not describe the sound of our bell, and it's a pity, a pity. You, gentlemen, of course, haven't yet read the *Trilogy*."

"I've read it, I've already read *With Fire and Sword*, and *The Deluge*, and *Pan Wołodyjowski*. I've read it," I wanted to call out, but I restrained myself and bit my tongue. My psychological instinct, not yet perfected, but already in place, whispered to me that demonstrating any sort of ability in the presence of Sexton Messerschmidt wasn't a good thing. He was without a doubt a virtuoso, a virtuoso bell-ringer. Perhaps he was also a virtuoso in other arts, but above all else, he was the sort of virtuoso who feels like a fish in water among ignoramuses.

"But alas, alas, alas," you could tell that Messerschmidt had perfected every intonational nuance of the story he was telling, "Mikołaj

Radziwiłł dies too soon, and a few decades later the brother Catholics take away from the brother Calvinists their, that is to say, our church. Truth be told, they regain it, but from the great perspective of history, minor historical details are unimportant. What happens now, however, is a minor historical detail that creates great history, not only history in the historical sense, but also history in the epic sense. What happens now, gentlemen?"

Sexton Messerschmidt tore his hands away from the rope for a moment. Snatched upward by the swinging Radziwiłł rhythm, it danced above us its desperate, violently jerky dance.

"What happens, gentlemen? Well, one dark Kiejdany night four gentry-men—history hasn't recorded their names, we only know that they were three Calvinists and one Lutheran—one gloomy night that heretical foursome takes Mikołaj Radziwiłł's bell down from the Kiejdany town church. They load it on a sleigh, cover it with hay and pieces of straw, and off they go. The team of six horses sets off into the depths of the dark and icy Commonwealth. Although they couldn't have measured it back then, the heavy frost is well below zero, and it causes the sleigh to glide nimbly over the Kiejdany high road. A seventeenth-century full moon, black forests, and white fields. Gentlemen, the history of that expedition awaits its epic poet. But—there is no reason to hide the fact—this would have to be a man at least as linguistically talented as Henryk Sienkiewicz. Just think, gentlemen, and above all try to give free rein to your completely Bolshevized imaginations. Four Protestants, four riders, not of the Apocalypse, rather four riders of the Gospel carry the Protestant bell on their sleigh across the frozen century. They don't know where to go. Maybe to Warsaw? To Leszno? To Lublin? Or maybe to Prussia, to Königsberg? They don't know the way, they have no destination, they know only that they must protect the sacred object. And all around them is darkness, cut-throats, Cossacks, Tatars, Turks, Swedes, riffraff, and savages. At the speed of lightning the news spreads along the route that our musketeers are carrying royal treasures. Ambuscades. Skirmishes. Adventures. In the course of one of them, one of the Calvinist brethren is mortally wounded. The mythical dramaturgy of this journey lies in the fact that its participants slowly peel away. The next Calvinist is an ecstatic enthusiast of aquavit. He swills, you should excuse the expression, like Mr. Trąba, only he swills more desperately. One night, his extremities warmed to excess, having imprudently fallen asleep, he freezes to death. The remaining duo takes part in the scene of fatal initiation described so many times elsewhere. Flakes of morning snow settle on the eyelids of their inertly lying comrade. They don't melt. His face becomes covered with a white scale, and no one will ever know whether our erstwhile comrade in faith and comrade in arms had brown eyes or blue eyes, or whether in his breast pocket rustled a letter jotted down in someone's very tiny hand, for whom he longed and from whom he had fled."

Sexton Messerschmidt was clearly moved by his own rhetoric. A tear glistened in his eye. He didn't even try to hide the fact at all.

"You gentlemen will forgive me," he said in a rough voice, reining in his own emotion, "but, as the Bolsheviks are wont to say, I'm a *ślioznyj czeławiek*, a tearful man. The third, the youngest of the Calvinists," he continued, wiping the tear with his sleeve and blowing his nose out on the floor, "the third, the youngest of the Calvinists, was undone by what will soon undo all of you as well: a hasty exchange of glances with a certain Catholic woman.

"A tavern in the vicinity of Częstochowa, and a widow tavern-keeper of impressive corporality, older than him by a few good years. At dawn, instead of setting off further, instead of further escorting the bell, he's cutting wood in the courtyard, carrying water, and claiming that he's discovered the meaning of life. Gentlemen! The meaning of life and a mixed marriage—this is like fire and water! You don't understand a thing now anyway. Any moment, you will tumble into the arms of alluring young papist girls, but the time will come when you will remember my words. Never mind. On the field of battle, that is, on the route of the journey there remains the final rider of the Gospel, the Augsburg Lutheran evangelical. The route leads, God guides him, further to the south. It is already the height of a luxuriant, sweltering spring. The sleigh was long ago replaced by horse and cart. He is alone on the sandy road. His fingers graze the surface of the bell, smooth like a Protestant girl's skin, and that freezing, dark Kiejdany night when they took the bell down from the tower, when, driven not only by a divine calling, they set off into the unknown—that time, so it seems to him now, is not of this world, and not of this life. Now the road leads upward, hill after hill, higher and higher, and finally—there it is. At his feet stretches the promised valley. Evangelicals busy themselves around their farmyards. Church choirs sing psalm after psalm. Birds fly up to the sky. Everywhere a good, amicable light shines forth. Hosanna.

"And in that manner," the Sexton's voice suddenly seemed to break off, and now he spoke entirely without conviction, "and in that manner my ancient ancestor reached the Cieszyn land. Let the middle bell sing!" he suddenly shouted, and there was no way not to think that with this shout he wished to drown out something that either had not yet been said, or that had already been said in excess. "I'll tell you the story of the middle bell another time, another time. For today it is enough for you to know that it was cast and offered to us on the personal instructions of King Charles XII of Sweden, who not only routed the Evangelical-Eater, Emperor Joseph I, but also wrung from him six churches of Grace! That's right. Six churches of Grace! Sagan—Żagan! Freistadt—Kożuchów! Hirschberg—Jelenia Góra! Landshut—Kamienna Góra! Militsch—Milicz! Teschen—Cieszyn! And now, and now," Sexton Messerschmidt readied himself for the finale, "and now let the great bell sing!"

Hearts rocked under cast-iron domes that beat for all their might in their own rhythm, even though it was all directed by Messerschmidt. His voice was entirely buried in their music. It seemed to us that we pulled the ropes, but it was they that pulled us up and let us down. We flew up, and we fell down, like apprentice angels. Sexton Messerschmidt told the entire unhearable story of the great Wittenberg bell.

"That's right, that's right. The great bell comes from the castle church in Wittenberg," Sexton Messerschmidt's gaping mouth dumbly told the tale. "The generous folk of Wittenberg made an offering of that bell to the oppressed folk of Cieszyn, so that they, listening to the very same tones to which our Reformer, Dr. Martin Luther, listened, might not grow weary in their reformatory zeal. That's right, that's right, gentlemen, the great bell rang in the tower of the castle Church of St. Paul. It rang on that cold October morning when our Reformer, with the help of a sixteenth-century hammer, nailed his ninety-five theses on the topic of indulgences to the church door. If you gentlemen will listen carefully," Sexton Messerschmidt turned his face upward, "if you gentlemen will listen carefully, you will hear that the passionate banging of the Lutheran hammer has settled forever in the tone of the great bell, and it echoes in it quite clearly even now. That is to say," in Messerschmidt's unheard narration there echoed an almost audible venomous accent, "that is to say, if you are pious, you will hear it. The impious, Bolsheviks, pagans, and other slayers of Catholic girls won't hear a thing. For the might of our bell is based not only on the fact that its tone surpasses other tones, but that it also absorbs other tones and records them in the abysses of its substance. That is the reason why it is said that all of our bells are Wittenberg bells, although we also have a Swedish bell and a Radziwiłł bell. But the great Wittenberg bell surpasses them, it leads them, it absorbs their voice, and it bestows its own voice upon them. Listen, listen, and you will hear, in the transparent, cold, October air (the first snows lurk in the clouds over Wittenberg), you will hear the banging of the irascible hammer, piercing the parchment with iron nails."

.

I strained my ears, I slowly dressed, and more and more clearly I heard blows that were, admittedly, not irascible, but regular and forceful. An inky glow filled the kitchen. Someone had screwed a deep blue light bulb, left behind by the Germans, into the lamp that was hanging over the table. Mr. Trąba stood on a stool and nailed a large gray blanket to the window frame with unexpected skill.

"A black-out like during the occupation, like during the occupation, Chief, only even stricter. *Verdunkelung sensu largo*. Stricter, because under the Germans we were younger and often, especially after we'd had a glass, hastier. Stricter," Mr. Trąba sighed heavily, "stricter, because we are passing from the phase of theoretical debate to the phase of *praxis*."

With the lightness of a youth, he jumped down from the stool and occupied his place at the table. First of all he glanced intently at Father, then, I suppose absolutely by chance, since after all he couldn't see me—I had hidden among the coats in the entryway, and I was spying through the crack of the open door—and so, absolutely by

57

chance, Mr. Trąba glanced in my direction, was silent for a moment, and then began to speak in an especially stifled but at the same time solemn voice.

"Chief. I will speak off the top of my head, since, obviously, I didn't make any notes. Notes in our case mean certain deportation. I believe I remember everything, and I'll be able to say everything. If, however, it should turn out that my memory, impaired by excessive doses of the world, should bring me to some reprehensible lapse, I insist you call it to my attention. Gentlemen!" Mr. Trąba took too copious a gulp of air, like an inexperienced swimmer, which made his theatrically altered voice resound even more strangely. "Gentlemen! Comrade Gomułka lives in Warsaw at 7 Frascati Street, on the second floor of a five-story building that was built in the twenties. Functionaries of the security police occupy one of the apartments on the ground floor. There are six of them. They take shifts, three at a time, to cover twenty-four hours. They are armed, of course, even though they are demoralized by the peace and shameful—that's right, *shameful*—renunciation of the tradition of uprising that has reigned in our land for years. Practically the entire time, yes, the entire twenty-four hours of their shift, passes in card play. Mostly they play poker, although one of the shifts prefers gin rummy or a game called 'tail,' about which I know nothing more. They play for high stakes, sometimes even for ten złotys per point. This proves conclusively that bribery as a means of attaining our goal no longer comes into consideration. Unless first, in order to acquire the appropriate means, we rob a bank, or even several banks. As you gentlemen know perfectly well, the great terrorists, both Asiatic and European, operated in this manner. I fear, however, that we can't afford to join this tradition in any strict fashion, to follow faithfully in the footsteps of the classics of terror. *Anyway*, as the English say. All the guards who watch over Comrade Gomułka's safety know the taste of alcohol perfectly well, to put it mildly. More often than not they take a few nips while on duty, which might seem to create the impression of carelessness and lack of responsibility. Gomułka, like every disciplinarian in a position of leadership who lacks even a hint of a sense of humor, combats every sociable frivolity connected with work with all severity. He himself reaches for the bottle rarely, and he must always have a reason for it, moreover a reason that is exceptionally solemn, which puts him in the category of alcoholic layman and makes me, personally, utterly disgusted by his person. As you gentlemen know perfectly well," in Mr. Trąba's voice there sounded the note, which I knew well, that heralded the genre of the selfless epic, "as you gentlemen know perfectly well, alcoholic laymen who drink exclusively for solemn reasons or on festive occasions belong to a despicable category. The true artist of spirits drinks exclusively without a reason and without an occasion. What is more, he avoids—like an aristocrat—the typical occasions on which common mortals plunge themselves into the swamp of unexpected transports. Gomułka gets drunk exclusively on New Year's Eve. I really don't know a manifestation of worse taste. That's not all. On New Year's Eve he gets drunk with exceptionally repulsive methodicalness. Namely, around 9:00 in the evening he makes his appearance in the ballroom (usually in the Palace of Culture and Science, if it is the 'Ball of the Working People,' or in the assembly hall of the Warsaw Polytechnic, if it is the 'Ball of the Citizens of the Capital'). He takes his seat at the head table, and he doesn't budge from the spot until midnight. With relish, bending his neck in that characteristic way of his, he observes the absolutely spontaneous (of course!) merry-making. He sips moderately at a first, then takes a second glass. He doesn't dance. When, however, the midnight hour strikes, the beast in him is awakened. True, not right away, for first he stands and raises a toast to the New Year: 'Comrades, Citizens, Working People. The passing year was a year of strenuous labor and further advancement of economic progress . . .' But as soon as he has finished his toast, the first secretary immediately marches off to battle. He begins to drink more. True, he drinks with repulsive methodicalness, but he drinks greedily, and with great strides he surrenders himself to the art of dance. He renders compliments. He takes active part in the choral singing of proletarian songs, and he finishes his merry-making around 6:00 in the the morning in a state of absolute alcoholic dementia. If not for the tiny detail that this is a man constantly divorced from reality, you could say that once a year Comrade Wiesław divorces himself from reality. I once planned . . ."

"Mr. Trąba," in Father's voice curiosity vied with irritation, "how, by God the Father, do you know all these pieces of information?"

"I drew them from the same source where you, Chief, draw so much knowledge." Smiling playfully, Mr. Trąba tapped his index finger on the huge sheet of newspaper that was spread out on the table. "I read this between the lines of *The People's Tribune*."

"Mr. Trąba," Father said with a smile that was full of admiration, "if it weren't for the fact that we are on duty, I would pronounce the ritual formula: that this is a beautiful phrase, and worthy of reward. This is one of your most splendid ripostes. You have my esteem."

"A thousand thanks, Chief. That's right. We're on duty, and there can be no talk of even a drop of alcohol. On the other hand, however, I have to say that I would feel a particular distress if one of my most subtle lines went without the reward it deserves, even if it were to have a somewhat smaller measure, let's say half. Second, the hour is so late that we can accept the notion that the proverbial glass takes on the function of the bracing mocha. Third, and most important, it is time, I believe, that the youngest participant in the action," Mr. Trąba clearly pointed in my direction, "attained knowledge of our secrets and initiation."

Father remained silent and didn't budge from the spot.

"Chief," Mr. Trąba said with his official voice, one well trained in its officialness, "what you heard wasn't the empty twaddle of your friend, rather the voice of your superior and the commander of this action. Have the goodness to appreciate the fact that, bearing your merits in mind, I do not use the word 'order,' but I also ask that such acts of insubordination not be repeated in the future."

Father obediently stood up from the table, went up to the sideboard, took out a bottle and glasses, and placed them on the table.

"Come, Jerzyk," Mr. Trąba beckoned in my direction, and I entered into the inky abyss of the kitchen on trembling legs.

I was certain that I would immediately hear the ghastly word "child." "Please don't involve the 'child' in this," Father would immediately say, or "The 'child'—absolutely not," or "The 'child' should be sleeping by now," or "He's still a 'child.'" But Father filled the glasses in silence. I sat down slowly on the white lacquered stool, which now was as if coated with a light blue varnish. And Mr. Trąba spoke further:

"Jerzyk, my man! That you are a man is universally known." Could it be that he knew what I had been up to with the angel of my first love? The panicky thought flashed through my head, but Mr. Trąba was clearly not interested in concrete details. "We will not, therefore, repeat the obvious and thereby trivialize the beginning of the ritual. Namely, as a man, Jerzyk, together with other men (contrary to appearances both your Father and I still deserve that appellation), you will have the chance to participate in a great patriotic act. But as a child"—there you have it! I thought, there you have it! I have divine gifts and outpace reality by at least half a step—"for, after all, even being a man, you still are—and what is more, you always will be—a child in various ways, if only in the sense of being the child of your parents; and so, as a child, Jerzyk, you will have a completely unique opportunity, which, already at the very beginning of life, will put you in an incredibly privileged position. Namely, as a child, Jerzyk, you will have the chance to crush the serpent's brow:

'Who, yet an infant, crushed the serpent's brow,
In youth will choke the centaur's breath,
Snatch victims forth from hell below,
And win heaven's laurels after death!'"

Mr. Trąba recited carefully, placing each accent and pause in its appropriate place. "Whether in your further life you skillfully exploit the opportunity given you, that is, whether you will choke, snatch, and win what you ought—that, Jerzyk, is your business. We are giving you the sort of opportunity that none of your cohort has. But now, raise your glass, Jerzyk." From the beginning of his oration, Mr. Trąba had held his glass behind the safe enclosure of his fingers. "And now, raise your glass and drink. We all know, gentlemen," Mr. Trąba arose and we with him, "what the first sip of alcohol means in the life of a man. Jerzyk, in order to avoid choking like a debutant, an image so favored in second-rate literature, proceed according to the following method: just before drinking, take in a modest amount of air—in other words, inhalation; then, drink up in one gulp, not breathing out, of course— in other words, non-halation; then, delicately but decidedly release the air—in other words, exhalation. This is the point: after drinking schnapps you must release the air from the body in order to make room there for more of it. Gentlemen—Jerzy, Stanisław," Mr. Trąba clinked glasses with us, and Father and I did the same, we clinked our glasses, "gentlemen, let the head of the tyrant fall. To our health and to the health of all our tyrannicidal colleagues, living and dead."

And we drank. And I drank. And it went as smoothly as could be. The transparent cloud of juniper berry vodka threaded its way among the shadows of my entrails, and there were upon it signs and prophecies, and there were in this first sip of mine the prefigurations of all my future sips. Recorded in it were all my future falls, bouts of drunkenness, bottles, glasses, retchings, all my future delirious dreams, all my gutters, counters, tables, bars, all the cities on the pavement of which my corpse would once repose. There were all the waitresses with whom I would place orders in my life. You could hear in it my incoherent babble, and in it my hands shook. Even my death, shrouded in a cloak made of nothing but bottle labels, sat there and laughed terribly, but I wasn't afraid in the least. And so I drank. The first power entered into me, and together with it came the first great bestowal of wings. I was able to do everything now. With one action I was able to solve a thousand complicated equations. With one motion I was able to summon a thousand protective angels. With one kick I could kick a thousand goals. With one gesture of my powerful hand, with one finger, I could grind Władysław Gomułka to dust. I glanced at the faces of Father and Mr. Trąba, masked with a light-blue glow, and I knew that the same mask graced my face, that on my hands (just as on theirs) were the light-blue gloves of the conspirator. I recalled Sexton Messerschmidt telling the story of divine sparks, light-blue like a gas flame. I looked with rapture at my hands, which were now not only the hands of the born bell-ringer, but also the hands of the hired murderer, mercenary, marksman.

"And if by some miracle I should succeed," Mr. Trąba's voice returned a feeling of duty to me, "even if by some miracle I should succeed, and if I should manage to get into his immediate proximity, I wouldn't be able to do it from close quarters anyway. I wouldn't strike him down with a stiletto, to say nothing of doing it with my bare hands. The physical repugnance that I feel for Comrade Wiesław would certainly paralyze me. With my bare hands I could destroy Comrade Mao. Gomułka—absolutely not. And besides, it's easier to kill from a distance . . ."

"It's easier to kill from a distance from the moral point of view, harder from a technical point of view." Father very rarely formulated such general maxims.

"Chief," Mr. Trąba shouted enthusiastically, "I am madly envious of the accuracy of that formulation. I'm madly envious, and at the same time I reward you."

Mr. Trąba filled the glasses—mine, however, he filled only half way, which hurt me terribly. The venomous thought of desertion and betrayal immediately flashed through my mind.

"One way or another, the operation will have to involve a sniper," said Mr. Trąba. "Unfortunately the use of firearms is out of the question. It's out of the question for a thousand various reasons, among which, however, one seems sufficient to me: namely, I don't know how to use a firearm. Yes," Mr. Trąba became gloomy, "on the list of my numerous inabilities, you will find this inability as well . . . And even if," he continued, full of melancholy disgust for himself, "even if, by some miracle we were able to acquire, let's say, a shotgun, all the same there's too little time for me to master the art of marksmanship with the required precision. In a word, gentlemen," Mr. Trąba's voice again became the voice of the seasoned field officer, "in a word, gentlemen, there remains . . ."

"In a word, gentlemen, there remains the bow." Father's voice vibrated with mad fury. "Mr Trąba, enough of these jokes. If this is what you want, I can say that I refuse obedience as of this moment, I leave the detachment, I refuse to carry out any orders whatsoever, I leave the army, I join civilian ranks. I can utter any one of these scurrilous formulas. And I utter," it seemed to me that the light-blue glow on Father's face lightened even further on account of his deathly paleness, "and I utter this formula, and I utter all these buffoonish formulas at once, and at the same time," Father grabbed the bottle from the table, "I suspend in perpetuity all rewards for even the most breathtaking phrases . . . You go beyond the bounds of taste." Father spoke a bit more quietly, but he didn't calm down at all. On the contrary, the fury constantly growing in him now seemed to stifle his voice. "The very idea of an assassination attempt, the very idea of an assassination attempt is a risky one. This whole story constantly questions itself. But now we have the nail in the coffin of all plausibility

. . . You, Mr. Trąba, offend this whole unhappy nation . . . Don't you know how debased people are? Don't you know that it *really is necessary to kill him*? And you? If you intend to kill him at all, before you get around to killing him, you'll talk yourself to death. Don't you understand this, or what?"

"I understand it, I understand it well," Mr. Trąba said with a hollow voice.

"Since you understand it, why in the world do you mock us with your toys? By a billion barrels of beer! An assassin with a bow! A policeman with a ladies' umbrella! Meanwhile people are being carted off to Siberia. Hi diddly dee, the bowman's life for me." Dots of foam appeared in the corners of Father's mouth. "With a bow! Or how about a sling-shot! Or how about just like that!"

And gathering monstrous momentum, Father threw the bottle with all his might. Whether the ostentatious gesture was inversely proportional to his strength, or whether the power of Mr. Trąba's hypnotic and redeeming gaze, which never left the bottle, was so great, or whether this was a rare conjunction of various coincidences—whatever it was, nothing happened. If there was a target, the projectile missed its target. The bottle made a short and remarkably slow flight in the direction of the window. The blanket blacking out the window deadened the blow. Like a plane on approach, it slipped down along the gray surface and, bouncing off the bench under the window, landed safely on the ground, and it drowsily, with its final impulses, rolled in the direction of my feet. For a moment we stared at it in silence, perhaps in fear that at any moment it would explode all the same and be blown to pieces, flow away in glass mixed with juniper vodka; or perhaps in the hope that some sort of energy or force would enter into it and that, as if turned by someone's invisible hand, it would twirl roguishly and illicitly? But nothing happened. It was quiet, and the bottle, filled with the feverish and silent tussling of light-blue lights, rested at my feet.

"Chief," Mr. Trąba's voice had taken on an atypically realistic tone, "Chief, I really will kill him. Not with a simple bow, of course. I intend to shoot him with an arrow from a Chinese crossbow."

Chapter V

WHEN I FINALLY UNDERSTOOD MY ROLE IN THE ATTEMPT ON THE life of First Secretary Władysław Gomułka, black flames of betrayal and shame flared up within me. It was a sultry August morning. Through the open window you could hear the missionary orchestra. I put on my Sunday clothing in a fury. I hurried. I intended to become a turncoat before the worship service started. I slipped out of the house furtively, with the slippery step of the traitor.

"My beautiful Jesus! Shining King of the world!" the members of the women's chorus sang in the garden by the church, and they glanced at me with contempt. The missionary musicians pulled their trombones from their mouths and, looking in my direction in reproof, began to whisper something to each other.

"Hallucinations, Jerzyk, those are hallucinations. Hallucinations caused by your panicky fear," I whispered to myself. I crouched, my steps became heavier and heavier, the black foam of fear rocked in my entrails more and more dangerously, and right by the Lutheran church I had to stop. For the first time in my life I understood that if I weren't given wings, I wouldn't be able to go a step further. Later on that conviction was to become more and more frequent. The number of actions I was unable to carry out without wings grew. Finally, I was unable to do anything in life without wings. Even now I must constantly give myself wings in order to write this story.

I looked around me, and although the selection was considerable for the beginning of the sixties, and although all the taverns—Piast and The House of the Spa and Café Orbis—all of them were already open, and although all three were within sight, the fact that I was a minor was an insurmountable obstacle. Manly shoulders are one thing, a manly voice is one thing, but there wasn't the least chance that one of the three waitresses—that Helenka Morcinkówna (Piast), Krysia Kotulanka (The House of the Spa), or Marysia Jasiczek (Café Orbis)—would offer me schnapps. And so, led by something other than my own will, I turned left and hastened my step, and shortly after passing the Market Square I knocked at the gate of Mr. Trąba's house, which was hidden in the shadow of the ski jump. No one answered. I pressed the door handle. The door gave way. From the depths, from the dark vestibule, came individual words stifled by feverish spasmodic breathing.

Mr. Trąba lay on an iron bed, which was standing in the middle of a huge chamber that was even larger than our kitchen. Except for the bed, and the bottle that was standing by the bed, there were no pieces of furniture or any other objects, nothing. Just the numbed vastness of the waters, the castaway adrift in the middle, and a bottle full of disastrous news. Blood oozed from Mr. Trąba's cut forehead. Saliva flowed from his lips as they parted again and again. The green army pants he wore were completely soaked. The room was in the grip of the deathbed odor of a body that was passively floating in all its substances, although it was, in fact, filled with only one substance. Mr. Trąba said something, whispered, gibbered nonsense, but at first I wasn't able to catch even a single word, not even one intelligible sound. Still, I strained. I mobilized my secret talent for guessing words that had not yet been spoken, and after a moment—to tell the truth, after a very long moment—I knew more or less what it was about. The key word in Mr. Trąba's delirious narration was the word "tea," and the entire narration was about love. It was the sentimental complaint of a man lamenting the fact that he couldn't drink tea at the side of his beloved, since she was drinking tea at the side of another. The whole thing abounded in innumerable digressions, unintentional interjections, and unintelligible ornaments. Perhaps the general thrust of the lament—that drinking tea at the side of one's beloved was the single dream in the life of a man—was a too-incessantly-repeated refrain, but, taking Mr. Trąba's state into consideration, everything came out amazingly fluently. After all, it was as it always was with him: the sense of his story was the basic, and perhaps the only, tie linking him with the world. The beloved's name didn't come up even once. Perhaps I wasn't able to guess it, or perhaps I didn't want to guess it. I produced a white handkerchief from the pocket of my Sunday clothes. I poured a little vodka on it from the bottle standing by the bed. I applied the dressing made in this fashion to Mr. Trąba's forehead, and I wiped the slowly drying blood.

He fell silent for a moment. He opened his lips wider. A stream of tawny saliva flowed down over the gray growth on his cheek. He sighed and raised his lowered eyelids. He looked at me with an unconscious glance, and he half-whispered, half-wheezed:

"You shouldn't see me like this, Jerzyk. I am in both moral and physical decay."

And he reached out his trembling hand for the bottle I was still holding, and I bent over him. I carefully placed the bottle on his lips, and he drank. Then, having pulled himself together somewhat, he looked at me. In fact, you would have to say that he examined my intent most carefully. In a flash he understood the elementary goal of my visit, and he said:

"Drink to my return to health, Jerzyk. Do this as quickly as possible, since I am expecting the arrival of the sister of mercy at any minute."

And indeed, the dose I drank didn't even have time to reach my spiritual parts, when the massive figure of Mrs. Rychter—the widow of old Mr. Rychter, the owner of the department store—suddenly appeared in the room, as if out of thin air, dressed in a beautiful flowery dress.

"Good day, good day," she shouted, accenting the word "good" extravagantly and enunciating it theatrically. She immediately began to run around Mr. Trąba's bed. She ran, waved her arms, and shouted

"Good! Good! Good! *Gut! Gut! Sehr Gut!* Good life! Good life! To good life!"

She ran, and time and again she raised and dropped her hands. She clasped and unclasped her hands. She thrashed the air with her arms. She also performed knee bends, full of unexpected stateliness and at full speed. She was like a mad gymnast who had decided to commit suicide by performing all the sequences of exercises known to her to her last breath.

"Positive thinking! Positive thinking!" she roared at the top of her voice. "A well-disposed attitude to the world!" she screamed like a buffalo with its throat cut. "A well-disposed attitude toward the world works wonders. In the monthly *America* I read an interview with a man who, thanks to his well-disposed attitude toward the world, came back from prostate cancer! Prostate cancer!"

•

For a good while I had been withdrawing step by step. I had already crossed the dark entryway, and finally I felt warmth and light upon my manly shoulders. If it were not for the fact that I well remembered Mr. Trąba's indubitable arguments about warmth and light as the indispensable attributes of Satan, perhaps it would have seemed to me that I was returning from hell to the earth. But since I remembered and—what is more—believed, I surveyed the demon-filled world without any illusions.

Grand Master Swaczyna glided with a decisive gait through the empty and cleanly swept Market Square, dressed in a faultlessly tailored light-blue suit. I had received wings, and I was already prepared to commit an act of betrayal, but my enlightened mind now began to play for time and to consider the fundamental question of whether there was any need for committing an act of betrayal. I was enveloped by the smell of the world's most expensive eau-de-cologne. I bowed. Grand Master Swaczyna politely returned my bow.

"A beautiful day, Jerzy, my good man, as beautiful as, excuse the expression, five hundred new złotys," he began the conversation with his perfect low voice.

"The dearest day in the world," I responded.

Grand Master Swaczyna looked at me with his splendid blue eyes—to match them he chose the most expensive blue shirts and the most expensive blue suits in the world—and he sighed in relief.

"Conversation with you, sir, my good Jerzy, is a true pleasure. If you don't mind, if you have a little time, let's look in on my shooting-gallery for a moment."

Grand Master Swaczyna winked perfectly, smiled dazzlingly, and added playfully:

"My shooting-gallery worth all the money in the world. After you, sir," and he offered his hand.

I turned around, and I caught sight of a spanking-new Citroën in the shadow of an old spreading willow tree. The sky-blue body had in it the intensity of the heavens of August.

"I brought it here from Warsaw yesterday. I crawled along all day long. I was afraid I would destroy the engine. I sold the Moskwicz for a small profit."

Grand Master Swaczyna jingled the keys. He opened the windows and doors. He wiped invisible dust from the dashboard with a chamois. He started the engine, and, with his head thrown back, like a director listening to the first notes of an orchestra, he listened to the music of the first revolutions. The interior of the car smelled of the eternal odor of nothingness delimited by matter. It was the odor of the most expensive bars, exclusive clubs, and elegant apartments, the odor of costly hotels, rare substances, and harmonious objects.

We drove along the river. The first vacationers were taking off their dresses, rubbing suntan lotion onto their shoulders, and carefully spreading out gray blankets on the grassy banks. Grand Master Swaczyna nervously adjusted the collar of his deluxe shirt time and again.

"More than one body worthy of attention will be brought to the light of day today. More than one, Jerzy." His intonation misled me. I was certain that immediately thereafter he would add the necessary conclusion, or that he would offer me unambiguous advice about life. But he unexpectedly fell silent, and having lost my concentration and irritated at myself, I was no longer able to guess where he was headed, what he had in mind.

"Is it true what people say about you?" I asked after a while.

"It depends which of the numerous legends that circulate about me you mean. Just what do they say?"

"They say," I started stammering, although I had sworn that I wouldn't stammer, "they say, that you are the richest man in the world."

Grand Master Swaczyna waved it off scornfully.

"What do you mean?" he said with distaste and irritation. "What do you mean? Don't believe every rumor you hear. The richest man in the world! That's a good one!" Grand Master Swaczyna was enjoying his own scorn and irritation. "The richest man in the world! I'm not even in the top ten!" Now he spoke quickly and forcefully, with the bitter sarcasm of a man who was conscious of his defeats in life. "Come on, I'm not even in the top ten. It isn't enough that I'm not there, I'm falling. To put it bluntly, I'm falling on my face. Last year I was number fifteen, but today I'm seventeen. That, among other things, was precisely what I wanted to check on in Warsaw. Do you realize, Jerzy, what it means to be number seventeen!? It means not to exist at all."

·

Flakes of green paint were falling off the brittle walls of the shooting gallery. Through the crevices in the crooked boards and battered sheet metal arose straight streams of light. In the depths, in the thick green shadow, stood rows of glass tubes, paper flowers, and matches. Cigarettes hung on invisible threads. Black-and-white photos of film stars, petrified candies, above that shields full of shots, in the corner a monstrous doll no one could win—you had to have seventy-two points from six free-hand shots in order to win it, a result that even an Olympic champion could never achieve.

Małgosia Snyperek sat on a stool outside that rickety pavilion, which, it seemed, would collapse with the least puff of air. She exposed her freckled little face to the sun. She had rolled up her sad little dress, which was sewn together from various mismatched fabrics, and you could see her paper-white thighs. She was startled at the sight of us, and putting her sackcloth gown and her indifferent hairstyle in order, she fled inside and attempted to lend an expression of business-like readiness to her happenstance features.

"How's business, Miss Małgorzata? How's business today?" Mr. Swaczyna asked in a friendly, but at the same time thoroughly official, tone.

"There hasn't been anyone yet. There hasn't been a single client."

"That's not good." Grand Master Swaczyna became concerned, and he put on such an air, executed such gestures, and spoke such that there was no way around it: Małgosia had no choice but to feel guilty. Even I felt guilty.

"Maybe this afternoon," I said without conviction, "maybe things will pick up a bit this afternoon, when people start to go to the summer festival."

"That's not good." Grand Master Swaczyna, immersed in his supposedly immense calculations, seemed to have heard nothing. "That's not good. That's not good at all. If things continue like this, I'll be reduced to begging. In short, I don't know what to do." He suddenly turned to me and spoke as if he expected real advice. "In short, I don't know what to do. Whether to sell the firm for a modest gain, or to remodel, or to lower prices . . . I don't know . . . I'll have to think about it. Today is not a day for final decisions."

In very carefully choreographed reverie, Grand Master Swaczyna slowly began to take off his jacket. He took it off, methodically folded it, and delicately placed it on a counter that had been worn shiny by the elbows of generations of shooters. Then, with equal calm, he began to roll up the sleeves of his shirt. He rolled them up, and he said with studied politeness:

"Miss Małgorzata, a weapon and ammunition, if you please."

And when Małgosia Snyperek handed him an air-rifle and placed a can full of shot before him, he stood for a long time with the gun in his hand, with the barrel turned upwards, and with hateful reflection he examined the un-hittable army of matches, sticks, and glass tubes that paraded in the depths of the shooting gallery. And then, with uncanny accuracy, he began to decimate the rickety-legged detachments. Splinters and pieces of glass, scraps of paper floated about in the air. After each shot, Grand Master Swaczyna raised up the weapon with a melodious motion and shouted triumphantly:

"Dress!"

"Blouse!"

"Skirt!

"Slip!

"Bra!

"Panties!

"Left sandal!

"Right sandal!

"Left earring!"

Małgosia Snyperek laughed like mad. She lost consciousness from laughing. She bent over spasmodically. Her skull dangerously crossed the line of fire time and again. She hysterically pressed her extended palms to her breasts and to her belly as if she were afraid that the unceasing gunfire would indeed tear her clothes from her. After a good while, and, as usual, with a delay—as usual, in such situations, only with a delay—I understood the perverse sense of this game, and I glimpsed what those two must have been seeing for a long time. I glimpsed how Małgosia Snyperek's dress floated from her body, how her underwear and jewelry abandoned her, and all the cheap silver and the exceedingly limp parts of her wardrobe, hit time and again by the mercilessly accurate shots of Grand Master Swaczyna, fell to the ground, and Małgosia stood there naked as the Lord created her, and I stared at her for all I was worth. Liquid lightning bolts ran through my body, and the tantalizing conviction that Lutheran girls, contrary to the eternally suntanned Catholic girls, have paper-white skin became fixed for all time in the depths of my profoundly flustered heart.

"I'll be late to church," I said with a weak voice.

"Right away." Grand Master Swaczyna hurriedly put on his jacket. "I'll take you there right away. Miss Malgorzata, I'll be right back. I'll take Jerzy, and I'll be right back. I'll not be attending church, unfortunately."

When we got into the car I realized that all the time I had been waiting for him to make some allusion to snipers, that more or less consciously I was expecting Grand Master Swaczyna to compare one of his accurate shots to some very famous assassin's shot. I was expecting that he would perhaps mention at a certain moment the name of First Secretary Władysław Gomułka, that in general, in some manner or another, he would make it known to me that he knows. But Grand Master Swaczyna majestically changed gears. With fantastic nonchalance he stuck his elbow through the open window and lazily explained to me the reasons why he had stopped going to church.

"The matter is not that I have lost faith, Jerzy. On the contrary. I have kept my faith. What is more, I have kept my childhood faith. It still seems to me, I am still certain, that the Lord God, the Thundering Old Man with the Gray Beard, never takes His eye off me for a minute. Of course, I maintain close contacts with the atheists who currently rule this country. They are such close contacts that some might say: Grand Master Swaczyna quite simply *belongs* to the circle of atheists who currently rule this country. But you know, Jerzy, the atheists will pass, whereas I, Grand Master Swaczyna, will not pass. Religious fundamentalists will start to rule this country, and I will maintain close ties with the religious fundamentalists. If the Czechs come here," he extended his hand in the direction of the border running along the peaks of the mountains, "I'll do business with the Czechs. If the Germans return, be my guest. When the Russkies notice that their empire is beginning to creak like a breaking ice floe, and when the Russkies begin to strengthen their power, spasmodically and in their death throes, I don't see any obstacles—we will make alliances even with the dying Bolsheviks. I tell you, Jerzy, let the Hottentots come here: I will also occupy a seat in their Hottentot High Council. The Lord God sees this, and the Lord God understands. The Lord God entrusted the visible world to man so that he might take it under his control and do business with everyone. The Lord God doesn't let me out of His sight for a minute, and the Lord God understands perfectly well why I don't attend our church. After all, for the love of God, the Lord God can't like it much either that the Apostle Paul depicted in our stained-glass window is deceptively similar to Vladimir Lenin. Did you notice that ominous similarity, Jerzy? Take a careful look—although, on the other hand, there is no need here for careful examination: the thing is glaringly obvious. As you know perfectly well, the patrons of our church, the Apostles Peter and Paul, are depicted in the stained-glass window. As far as the Apostle Peter is concerned, everything is in perfect order: a handsome, mature man of Levantine looks, a fisherman's net on his shoulder, the raised right hand points to the lamb entangled in thorns, fine. But Paul, my favorite Biblical writer . . . His raiment, fine. The pilgrim's staff in his hand, fine. The other hand raised in the direction of the cross, fine. Everything is fine, with the exception of the head. For the figure of the Apostle Paul is crowned with a head that looks for all the world like Vladimir Ilyich Lenin. And that, Jerzy, is troublesome. Who cares about the identical bald pate? After all, all bald men look alike. But here we have the same features, the same slanted Asiatic eyes, the same cheekbones, the same cut of the beard . . . Come on! . . . You know, Jerzy, at first I thought this might mean something . . ."

The Grand Master fell silent for a moment. With lifeless attention he stared at three unusually comely women tourists running down the steep bank to the water.

"I thought this might mean something, for there was a calamitous period in my life when it seemed to me that art meant something. I've read a lot in my time, and the Fine Arts have also excited my curiosity. Not entirely disinterestedly, to tell the truth. It seemed to me, for example, that who knows whether the furious rhythm of the inflow and the outflow of money isn't recorded in works of art, in those works that, so it seemed to me, were inspired, that outpaced reality. Incidentally, that rhythm has certainly been noted in the most outstanding works, for example, in *The Magic Mountain* or *Ship of Fools*, but be that as it may. It's impossible that this was a coincidence, that's what I think: that distinctively enlarged skull of the leader of the revolution on prominent display in the Evangelical stained-glass window—that can't be a coincidence. Especially since the artist and glass-painter, may his name be forgotten for all time, created his work in the thirties. If only that was some sort of cretin, a petty fiddler with a narrow specialization. Nothing of the sort! This was a man of wide horizons and broad interests. He painted, sculpted, wrote. And I, poor sucker, began to ask myself what that man wanted to express through his audacious aesthetic conception. I began to investigate the matter. It seemed to me, for example, that the Asiatic-Leninist head of the Apostle Paul might be some sort of allusion to Luther. For you know, Jerzy, not to take anything away from our Reformer—but the old boy wasn't a looker. Have you read *The Magic Mountain*?"

I shook my head.

"Read it. That is reading matter for which it is never too early or too late. When you read it, you will come upon a fragment in which

Mr. Settembrini says the following to Hans Castorp. I know the passage by heart. And so, Mr. Settembrini says the following: 'Look at him, this Luther! Observe the portraits we have, in early and later life. What sort of cranial formation is that, what cheek bones, what a singular emplacement of the eye! My friend, that is Asia!' Yes, Jerzy, take a good look at Luther. That's a powerful piece, a powerful fragment, considering that Thomas Mann was a Lutheran. Although one ought rather to say that there was, that there lived in this world, a Lutheran who was Thomas Mann. I doubt that this was good for Lutheranism. In any case, I followed that Asiatic trail, I investigated, I studied, I made enquiries, I interpreted, and do you know what? It turned out that the likeness of the Apostle Paul with the head of Lenin that you can see in our church is the result of chance, ignorance—although, for all that, no less shameful! The guy simply didn't know what Lenin looked like! And not only that, in the year of our Lord one-thousand-nine-hundred-and-thirty-two the guy had no idea that, just a few hundred kilometers from here, the Bolshevik Revolution had taken place! Not a clue about God's good earth, nothing but high art. Botticelli, Rubens, and Rembrandt; Chopin, Schubert, and Schumann. Which is a good thing. But I think, Jerzy, that if someone doesn't know what Lenin looks like, he shouldn't get it into his head to paint the Apostle Paul. That's what I think."

"But by what miracle did he paint it, granted not where he ought to have, and yet, he painted it—Lenin's head. By what miracle did he do that, if he had never seen Lenin's head?" I was amazed by my own shrewdness.

"Oh, by some sort of diabolical miracle, by some connective tissue in the painter's subconscious. If you don't want to paint Lenin, you have to know what Lenin looked like, because otherwise an unpleasant surprise may come your way. That's right, Jerzy. In any case, this is the fundamental reason why I stopped going to our church. You know, I spend too much time in rooms adorned with portraits of Ilyich to have to experience it in church too, such—let's be clear about this—such *mixed* feelings. When once or twice a year I feel the irresistible urge to visit the House of God, I drive to Ustroń and *fertig*. And besides, I've clearly become disgusted by art. I'll say more: I despise art. I know that this sounds quite barbaric, but I've come to the conclusion that guys who don't know the current prices of basic articles of consumption, as well as the current exchange rate of the dollar, are not in a position to tell me anything about the world, not in their poetry, not in their painting, not in their music. It is possible that an unearthly spirit speaks through them, but, because of their earthly laziness, they are not prepared to fully understand the language of that spirit. I repeat. I'm aware that this is unfair, but I, Grand Master Swaczyna, adhere to this rule: three times a year I drive to the church in Ustroń, and once a year I read *The Magic Mountain*, and that is nourishment sufficient unto my soul. Amen, amen, Jerzy. Run along now, the service is just starting. Run, and pray. Praise the Lord with your singing of Psalms, and don't glance too frequently in the direction of the stained-glass window."

I was already getting out of the car, already the missionary music was enveloping me. Female choralists were singing, the Wittenberg bells were ringing, Protestants were gathering. I was just about to cross the cold shadow of the high church walls when Grand Master Swaczyna leaned out of his car and called to me once again:

"Jerzy, I beg your pardon, but I almost completely forgot about a most urgent matter. Please be so kind as to relate to your father, the Chief, that the object about which we spoke, your father will know what it is about—you, too, after all—please tell your father that I ordered a prototype made in one of my workshops."

The Grand Master examined me carefully. He measured me with his glance from head to foot, and he added with deadly gravity:

"Don't worry, Jerzy. You'll look fantastic with a crossbow on your shoulder."

•

I didn't sing the Psalms, I didn't listen to the sermon, not once did I look in the direction of the front wall, which was almost entirely covered with the watery colors of the stained-glass window. I sat with lowered head. I prayed, and I definitely drove away the chimera of betrayal. In passing, and perhaps not at all in passing, Grand Master Swaczyna had said the decisive thing; he gave name unceremoniously to the hope that was vaguely sprouting in me: that, striding through the streets of Warsaw with a crossbow on my shoulders, I might indeed attract the attention of women.

"Women and men, children and old geezers. Everybody," Mr. Trąba had sought to convince me, and to the extent that, on that first occasion, I listened to his arguments in our darkened kitchen with growing animosity and an ever stronger will to betrayal, now I repeated those same arguments to myself, word for word, in a spirit of meekness and understanding. Even then I was incredibly keen about my own seductiveness.

"I know one green tree, beautiful the olive tree. There the nightingale sweetly sings to our beloved psaltry," sang the women's chorus. I raised my head slightly. I stared at them just as shamelessly as I had at Małgosia Snyperek a few moments before. The second from the left was alluring like a Canaanite woman. "Or I will hasten away into the first faint light with a Canaanite woman, To search through the land of Galilee for the grace of heaven," I sang together with her, and together with the tempting Samaritan woman, fifth from the left, and together with the raven-haired Philistine woman in the middle, and I humbled myself before the Thundering God, the Old Man with the Gray Beard, and the words of the hymns got mixed up in my head with the words of Mr. Trąba. "Or I will go with that Samaritan woman at midday joyfully, Where over Jacob's well the nightingale warbles wondrously." I will go at midday joyfully, Gomułka to kill wondrously, I joked, and I sang in spirit, and the specter of betrayal vanished definitively, and I came to understand in the process that the harmonizing of rhyme and truth in poetry is not an easy thing: after all, the death-bearing shaft was to pierce the heart of the First Secretary not at midday but in the evening.

According to Mr. Trąba's plan, we were going to wander boldly around the streets for the entire day, taking in the sights of the capital; we were going to climb to the top floor of the Palace of Culture quite openly, go to the Old Town, and ride to "Decade of Socialism" stadium; we were going to move about with ostentatious openness and absolute freedom; we were going to proceed this way, since, so Mr. Trąba was assuming, no one would remember us anyway, since no one would look at us anyway, since, anyway, all would be examining me, Jerzyk, and not even so much me, Jerzyk, as my peculiar plaything, the crossbow strapped to my shoulder. And even if someone should glance at me, he wouldn't for the world be able to identify me the next day, because I will be distinctly and unrecognizably disguised. My cheeks will be covered with venomous war paints, on my head I'll have a luxuriant headdress, I'll be wearing a broad caftan that will alter my silhouette and at the same time draw attention with its gaudy colors.

"Gentlemen, it's perfect!" Mr. Trąba choked on his own saliva. "There's no gap in this plan, not a crack. This isn't some sort of extravagance in the plotline. It's just clear-sighted rationalism and strict adaptation to the requirements of the circumstances. We have to go to Warsaw on the night train that leaves here at 10:17 in the evening and has a scheduled arrival of around 7:00 in the morning. We have to—yes or no?"

Only now did I realize that Mr. Trąba's "yes or no," so imperious and impervious to dissent, was riddled with desperate uncertainty.

"Other more circuitous itineraries, with a number of different trains, don't come into question, since a journey like that would last a few days and maybe even a week. Yes or no? In order to avoid problems with Station Master Ujejski we will force our way into the postal ambulance car, and we will ride in the company of the guards, who until recently were serving under your command, Chief, and who are now your friends. Yes or no? Yes."

Such were the assumptions that defined the time and conditions of our expedition to the capital. From these assumptions arose—irrefutably, in Mr. Trąba's opinion—the following conclusions. Even if our train were to reach Warsaw Main Station punctually, that would all the same be the time when Comrade Gomułka, seated in the rear of a black Volga, accompanied by his personal secretary, Józef Tejchma, and with a motorcycle escort of militiamen armed to the teeth, would be making his way along the following streets: Prus, Konopnicka, Wiejska, and Nowy Świat, in the direction of the headquarters of the Central Committee. Even if we were to take up the absurd and suicidal idea of attacking the armed convoy, we simply wouldn't make it on time. It goes without saying that no one in his right mind would make an attack upon the Central Committee itself. *Ergo*, we will have to spend the entire day in Warsaw. Theoretically, we could hide in the apartment of one of his *numerous*—so Mr. Trąba assured us—Warsaw acquaintances, hide and wait the dozen hours, but from the psychological point of view this would be a cardinal error. Mr. Trąba referred to the many testimonies and memoirs of old terrorists that he claimed to have studied carefully. It followed from them irrefutably, so he claimed, that the worst and most calamitous thing for assassins was inactive waiting around for the zero hour. If they waited too long, they became demoralized and lost their concentration. Their nerves went on the fritz. Mr. Trąba also made it known in a circuitous but still sufficiently clear fashion that, in his case, the unbearable vacuum of some dozen hours of waiting could be filled and made to pass quickly only in a manner that was—although typical for him—undesirable.

"We can't risk any sort of inefficiency. As it is, there are too many improvised elements in our whole enterprise, and we are not going to repeat the historic errors of old assassins. We will spend the final hours before we kill Gomułka touring the city." Mr. Trąba emphasized this aspect many times, and I, Jerzyk, now listening raptly to the words and melody of old Lutheran Psalms, not only agreed with him, but I also admired his unshakable logic.

"When once I erred around the forest unhappy, suddenly I heard a voice from the thick branches of the olive tree. When I rested in its shade, and began to ponder that song in my heart, I arose refreshed," sang the choir of Canaanite, Samaritan, and Philistine women. And indeed, in my simplicity, refreshed by the assent to everything that had filled me, I raised my head even higher, and above the divine coifs of the women's chorus, I glanced at the stained-glass window, filled with undulating light, at the figures of the apostles looming from the exploding radiance, and there was in me no bitterness, distaste, or disappointment. My transaction with Grand Master Swaczyna was ultimately a spiritual transaction, and what is more I, Jerzyk, knew the rules of that transaction well. After all, I well knew, and had known for a long time, that neither in the figure depicted on the glass, nor in the shape of the head, nor in the likeness of the countenance of the Apostle Paul was there the least hint of similarity to Vladimir Ilyich Lenin.

Chapter VI

Elżunia Baptystka knew the answer to every question. She knew how many crosses there were in our church and what adorned and crowned the pulpit; what the first miracle performed by Lord Jesus was and when the Descent of the Holy Spirit took place. She was even able to give the precise number of all the books of the Bible and the date of Pastor Potraffke's ordination. Dressed in white stockings and a green woolen frock, Elżunia won the church trivia contest year after year. She would confidently ascend the podium and resolutely answer the questions posed by the presbyters. The Pastor's Wife would kiss her on both cheeks and present her with edifying literature. I hated Elżunia Baptystka. And I lusted after the Pastor's Wife.

Then it was my turn. I stepped through the high October grass on trembling legs. I climbed the podium that had been cobbled together out of pine planks, breathed in the scent of the shiny wood, glanced at the festive crowd seated below, at the giant rock by which the Lutherans of old used to gather in times of persecution. I glanced at the beech forest surrounding the glade, and I felt on my palate the watery taste of disaster. The Curator of the Church Grange glanced playfully at the Pastor's Wife, then with pretended reflection he fixed his gaze upon me and said:

"And now, a question from the field of the life of our parish. Please tell us the style and color of the Pastor's Wife's favorite hat!"

Of course I knew perfectly well that the Pastor's Wife's favorite hat was a red and black toque with a pompom on the side. I knew the Pastor's Wife's wardrobe inside and out. I knew what her favorite skirts, frocks, and blouses were. I knew how she dressed for every time of the day and season of the year. I even knew how many pairs of flat-heeled pumps she had. I knew everything, but, of course, I remained silent. I didn't yet have a clue how one ought to behave in the presence of women after whom one lusted, but my instinct, as blind and as powerful as my lust, whispered to me that, in any case, you ought not to hold forth about their wardrobe in their presence. I remained silent. The Pastor's Wife looked at me with ostentatious coldness and indifference. Her gaze went through me as if I weren't there. Suddenly I understood that her glance was too cold, too indifferent, that she looked at me as if I weren't there because I was . . . Jesus Christ, she loves me! I experienced a sudden revelation, and the apparently disparate elements—every glance, chance meeting, and meaningless phrase—arranged themselves, in the twinkling of an eye, into a complete whole. "The Pastor's Wife is madly and unhappily in love with me," I slowly and thoughtfully repeated this sentence to myself—just like vodka, it lent me wings, and indeed I felt myself take wing, that I could answer. What was more, I would answer each question exhaustively and ornately.

I hadn't a clue how to act in the presence of a woman who was madly in love with me, and I fell subject to the thoroughly male delusion that, in the presence of a woman who was madly in love with you, you can allow yourself everything.

"In that case," the Curator again looked playfully at the Pastor's Wife and again with feigned reflection fixed his gaze upon me, "in that case, the next question from the same field. This one is more difficult. When the Pastor's Wife directs our choir, what characteristic gesture—in no way connected with directing—does she make, especially at rehearsals?"

I glanced at her. Mercilessly, I sought out her panicked, fleeing glance, and I spoke slowly, luxuriating in my own omniscience:

"Before she begins to direct—although some times, sporadically, it happens after the choir has performed the first hymn—the Pastor's Wife takes three silver bracelets off her left hand and she places them on the director's side-table next to the music stand. She always places them in the same fashion, such that the intersecting circles of the bracelets divide the surface of the side-table into eight separate regions. At the end of rehearsal, the Pastor's Wife puts the bracelets back on, reversing the order in which she had taken them off. This means that first she puts on the bracelet that's on the very bottom, the one with the small ruby on the clasp, next the one with the black Aztec design, and finally the chain-form wristlet . . ."

There was a moment of utter silence. The birds fell quiet. Nature came to a standstill. Not even the shadow of the simple thought that maybe I had gone a bit far passed through the limited brain of this class genius. I luxuriated in my infallibly A+ answer. I also luxuriated in the fact that only I, her wise beloved, could see the imperceptible blush that was slowly covering her dark cheeks. The Pastor's Wife's complexion was not white like paper; it was dusky like the Rose of Zion, like the shoulders of King Solomon's betrothed. The Pastor's Wife was dark like the consort of a Brazilian soccer player. Thunderous applause erupted, rousing a black grouse at the edge of the forest to a fluttering run. Everyone who was sitting at the table, made of the same pine planks as the podium, clapped. Father, Mother, and Mr. Trąba clapped—admittedly, with a peculiar reserve; but the rest, with the exception of Father Pastor Potraffke—I don't know how he clapped because, of course, I didn't dare to look at him—all the rest, Grand Master Swaczyna, Małgosia Snyperek, Sexton Messerschmidt, Mrs. Rychter, Commandant Jeremiah, and even Elżunia Baptystka, and all the confirmation students sitting below at a table of their own, all clapped as was proper.

I sat down among them, placed the edifying literature in front of me, and drank a sip of soda pop that was green like the Orinoco.

"Brothers and sisters," said Father Pastor Potraffke, "let us return to the subject of our dispute."

"Which one?" Mr. Trąba asked. "Killing Gomułka?"

"The killing of tyrants in general," replied Father Pastor Potraffke with impatience in his voice. "If it is a question of killing Gomułka, then why, basically, do you need to kill him, since Communism will collapse sooner or later anyway?"

"If the comrades kill the Comrade First Secretary, the system will collapse later, and perhaps it won't collapse at all," Commandant Jeremiah's voice thundered ominously and menacingly. "Comrades, you wish to speed history up, but with your irresponsible escapade—incidentally, I don't believe in its realization, and that's the only reason why I take part in this academic discussion—with your irresponsible escapade you will slow history down. That is inconsistent with the spirit of revolution."

"I don't intend either to speed history up or to slow it down," Mr. Trąba spoke more quietly than everyone else, as if led even now by the modesty that ought to characterize the Chief Assassin. "I don't intend either to speed it up or to slow down. I intend to lend it a definitive character. Or rather to make society aware of the inevitability of history. Perhaps the Communists, deprived of their leader, will not disperse but will close ranks instead, causing the system to last a little longer, but the inevitability of the end will be all the more evident."

"Personally, it seems to me," the television announcer's voice of Grand Master Swaczyna resounded, "personally, it seems to me that the role of doing away with scoundrels is not for a serious person who has other, more serious things to do in this world. It should be left to frustrated and penniless students. Let them throw bombs at the feet of tyrants."

"We are all Protestants," said the Curator of the Church Grange, "and Protestants are supposed to shine by example."

"I am," Mr. Trąba slowly measured out every word, "I am, in a certain sense, a frustrated student without a penny to my name, and I have nothing more serious to do in this world. I am also a Protestant, and I wish to shine by example."

Sexton Messerschmidt had been fidgeting for a good while.

"Be that as it may," he said with irritation, "be that as it may, it's getting time to begin the second part of the banquet. It's getting cold."

Grand Master Swaczyna bowed, with unusual politesse, in Sexton Messerschmidt's direction, and he said soothingly:

"A moment of patience, a moment of patience. I placed a suitable order, and it will certainly be delivered any moment."

"Protestants have never taken part in assassinations." The Pastor's wife descended from the podium and sat down at the end of the table, as far away from me as possible.

"Protestants never took part in anything at all," Father muttered sullenly. "Not taking part is the chief characteristic of Protestants, especially in Poland."

"I've told you a thousand times," Mr. Trąba chimed in even more quietly and with even greater forbearance, "I've told you a thousand times that if someone doesn't exist at all, it's hard for him to take part in anything."

"But comrade, you intend to take part in the killing of Gomułka, and an active part at that," Commandant Jeremiah shouted triumphantly.

"Active and definitive. As a Protestant, who doesn't exist, I can kill without hesitation, since the act will remain in the realm of nothingness. If, as some say, Poland is a Catholic country, then, there you have it! It follows clearly from this that, if *lèse-majesté* is perpetrated in a Catholic country by a non-Catholic, that is by nobody, or by a foreigner, then the good name of our holy fatherland, the holy mother of all fatherlands, to whom the tradition of assassinating kings is foreign, will remain unsullied, and at the same time she will gain the name of the one who, as the first of the oppressed, raised her hand against the usurper. You don't appreciate the precipitous dialectic of my patriotism."

"Once again it's the Catholics who are to be blamed for everything." Pity struggled for supremacy with barely suppressed fury in Station Master Ujejski's voice. "Once again it's the Catholics who are to be blamed for everything. I swear, every time I accept your heretical invitation to an allegedly ecumenical vodka-bibbery, I always discover that it's the Catholics who are to be blamed for everything, and as a Catholic—a sorry example, but still a Catholic—and yet, as the Catholic, I end up looking like an ass. It's inconceivable that in a Catholic country a tiny handful of apostate brethren should make a fool out of any Catholic, even me. We aren't to blame; you're to blame. You shouldn't have made a schism."

"Mr. Ujejski," Sexton Messerschmidt raised his voice, "you shouldn't have brought about the crisis of the papacy in the Middle Ages. You shouldn't have dealt in indulgences."

"If you really think," the Station Master replied coldly, "if you really think that I, Tomasz Ujejski, son of Tomasz, brought about the crisis of the papacy in the fifteenth century, as well as dealt in indulgences, then you, Mr. Messerschmidt, were right to reform the Christian Church."

"Of course I was right," the Sexton shouted.

"You're always right, because your 'right,' all of your heretical 'right,' is by definition greater than logic," said the Station Master dismissively.

"It all comes from an improper diet and a lack of optimism." Mrs. Rychter's tone seemed to herald an extensive lecture on the topic of healthy food and a positive attitude, but Sexton Messerschmidt, clearly subject to the changing mood, interrupted her with unexpected enthusiasm:

"Very well said. I'd like to consume something that would give me optimism. Business is business, but optimism is optimism."

"Brothers and sisters," said Pastor Potraffke, and he raised up his arms.

In the depth of the forest a car horn resounded. Grand Master Swaczyna glanced at his watch. A rapturous smile lit up Sexton Messerschmidt's face. The grimace of a painful contraction flitted across Mr. Trąba's countenance. An army jeep appeared at the end of the forest road, and, rocking on the ruts, it slowly drove up to the middle of the glade.

"Permit me to propose a modest repast," said Grand Master Swaczyna. He stood up from his place and moved in the direction of the vehicle, stopped for a moment, and, turning back in Station Master Ujejski's direction, added: "A modest ecumenical repast."

•

It was never like that again. White planets began to glide along the darkening horizon, stars were falling just behind our backs. The missionary musicians ascended the podium, and they began to play old

85

Austrian marches and waltzes. Waiters in white coats with gold buttons carried chains of hunters' sausage on silver platters. They placed before us bottles of Żywiec, Pilsner, and vodka, mustard in great jars, and home-baked bread on wicker trays. Four bonfires burned in the four cardinal directions. Light flowed through beer mugs and prewar chalices made of massive glass. The Pastor's Wife pretended she didn't see me. Elżunia Baptystka didn't let me out of her sight.

"Elżunia," I said to her, "I'm not in love with you."

"Oh, love!" retorted Elżunia. "That doesn't really happen."

"It happened to me."

"The blonde? The married woman who rented a room from Mrs. Rychter on the fifth floor? Little boys often think they're in love with grown women, but even if it's their first love, it usually isn't true love."

"This is true love. When I grow up, I'm going to marry her."

"Jerzyk, first she would have to divorce her husband."

"She will do it," I said with absolutely charming certainty.

Elżunia giggled, but almost immediately her slightly asymmetrical features, ones that foretold incredible beauty, went into disarray. At that time, I didn't yet know that speaking with a woman with whom you are not in love about another woman with whom you are in love is a deadly transgression, but I remembered the expression on Elżunia Baptystka's face forever. It was not an expression of despair, or pain, or even of distaste. It was an expression of slowly mastered vulnerability. It was the look of the helpless woman who is trying to come to terms with male thoughtlessness, since there is nothing else to be done. Elżunia Baptystka got the better of my thoughtlessness and said:

"Before she divorces her husband for you, before you grow up, at least visit her. When you go to Warsaw in November with your father and Mr. Trąba to kill Gomułka, drop by and see her, while you have the opportunity."

She looked me in the eyes and added:

"You're very amorous, Jerzyk. Grow up as quickly as possible. Amorousness combined with erotic illiteracy is a deadly combination."

I was certain that she would say something about the Pastor's Wife just then. I was so irrefutably certain of it that I was feverishly working on a ruthless and brutal answer that would strike her to the quick, but Elżunia pointed to the edge of the glade and said:

"There they are, Jerzyk. They have returned, because they can't live without you."

As narrators of old used to say, I rubbed my eyes in amazement. At the edge of the forest, on the outskirts of the glade, on the border between radiance and darkness—there stood the morphinistes. They had lightened their hair and let it grow out. They were not wrestling with their Babylonian blanket. They had thrown broad men's jackets made of quilted nylon over their shoulders. They were thus, especially to my unskilled eye, changed beyond recognition. But there they were.

"Yes, it's them," Elżunia Baptystka dispersed the shadows of my doubts, "it's them, the morphinistes, otherwise known as Anka and Danka. Of course they aren't morphine addicts. They are psychology students, and shortly they'll begin to write their master's theses. One of them will write about the psychology of a woman who is waiting for a man, and the other about the psychology of a man who is waiting for a woman. Run to them as fast as you can, my sweet lover boy."

I had the irresistible urge to do so, but something beyond the sensory realm told me that if I set off in an ecstatic rush, I would make an utter fool of myself in front of Elżunia. I had all the greater urge for that mad, welcoming rush, since everyone had noticed them now, and everyone (strictly speaking—all the men) was already running in their direction. Even Father, even Father ran nimbly through the high, dark-blue grass. Or if he wasn't running, he was walking with a very hurried step. Mother, the Pastor's Wife, and Małgosia Snyperek stood up from their places and observed the welcoming ovations with gloomy faces, but I took Elżunia by the hand, and, with a dim presentiment that occupying the last place in the popular game of appearances wasn't a bad thing, I said:

"Come on, Elżunia, let's go greet them."

She looked at me with a suddenly brightened gaze and whispered:

"Well, you learn quickly. That's comforting."

•

We embraced them, kneeled before them, squeezed their divine hands. They were beautiful. In their faces, slimmer now and flogged by Lutheran winds, there wasn't a trace of the old defects. They were beautiful, but oddly abashed. They kept looking around, whispering something, exchanging knowing glances, behaving as if they were waiting for something or someone. And indeed, when, after a short while—so short that no form of their further being had had time to emerge after the chaotic greeting—male choral singing resounded in the nearby thickets, they smiled with obvious relief.

"Our boyfriends," said one of them.

"Our Czech boyfriends are drawing near and singing," added the other.

The singing became louder and louder, the words of the songs more and more distinct: "Yesterday I was at the dance, at the dance all day," the invisible Czech boyfriends of the morphinistes sang, and when they became visible, it didn't surprise any of us that there were five of them; five choristers, handsome as Czech hockey players, came out into the glade and sang: "My blue-eyed girl, I didn't grind, I didn't grind, the water took our mill;" then they sang "To a Circle, a Circle" and "Slavonice Polka." They sang beautifully and sonorously in five beautiful and sonorous voices, and they didn't interrupt their singing of the old Czech songs for even a moment. They sang "Beer Barrel Polka" and "Wedding Ring" and "Treacherous Hošíček." We invited them to join us at the table. Grand Master Swaczyna delivered a welcome address that was filled with heartfelt internationalism, and the inspired singers, dressed in dark-green track suits, walked across the meadow and sang: "Shepherdess Annie, You Don't Have a Fiddle at Home" and "My Charlie," and they sat down at the table and sang "We Won't Get Up in the Morning on Time" and "The Time has Long Passed." And then they sang, "Where beer is brewed, there we prosper. Where beer is drunk, there we thrive. Let us go there and drink" until the foggy autumn dawn, and our unending dialogue about killing was conducted throughout that sweltering and holy night to the lively accompaniment of their singing. "I planted a convally, but a lily grew."

·

Father Pastor Potraffke raised up his arms and said, or rather, shouting over the singing Czechs who were deaf to everything but their own song, he cried out:

"It was as it was, but one always somehow muddled through; but for us Protestants it was sometimes neither the one way nor the other. More precisely, it often is neither the one way or the other for us. On the one hand, in the twelfth chapter of the Epistle of St. Paul to the Romans, we find the pertinent commentary concerning absolute civic obedience toward the higher authority. On the other hand, it isn't true that Protestants haven't ever taken part in assassinations . . ."

"The Apostle Paul writes about authority that comes from God. If Gomułka's authority comes from God, I fear I'll lose my faith," said Sexton Messerschmidt acidly.

"In the first place, the apostle says that every authority comes from God," Father Pastor Potraffke interrupted him, and with a gesture of his hand he quieted the polemicists who were ready with immediate ripostes. "I agree. I agree, that it is doubtless a matter here of true authority, and that the false, usurpatory authority of the brother Communists does not come from God. But the Fifth Commandment, brothers and sisters, does come from God, and there are no exceptions to it."

"Maybe you don't make any exceptions, but we do. This is the basis of our superiority over you. The Catholic Church is the Church of elastic intellectuals, and your Lutheran Church is the Church of dogmatic doctrinalists," Station Master Ujejski smiled venomously.

"People, hold me back, or I'll have to remind him of the Second Schmalkaldic War," cried out Sexton Messerschmidt.

"He who lacks arguments resorts to fisticuffs," said Station Master Ujejski in a voice that vibrated with rage, though it was still rather calm. After a moment, however, fury took possession of him entirely. He leaned out in the direction of the Sexton and began to hiss hatefully: "The Battle of White Mountain didn't teach you a thing, it didn't teach you a thing! St. Bartholomew's Night didn't teach you a thing . . ."

"Brothers, calm yourselves!" cried out Father Pastor Potraffke. "Let the spirit of peace reign between you!"

And after a moment, as if wishing to reinforce the spirit of peace with the sprit of sobriety, he turned to Station Master Ujejski:

"What sorts of exceptions do you have in mind? What exceptions can there be to the Fifth Commandment?"

"Thomas Aquinas answers the question whether it is possible to grant dispensation from the Ten Commandments in the affirmative: it is possible to grant dispensation," replied Station Master Ujejski, now with a calmer tone, "because the Commandments belong to natural law, and natural law is sometimes fallible, and thus it is possible to grant dispensation."

"The Commandments are established by God, thus I think only God could grant dispensation from them," said the Pastor's Wife, shrugging her shoulders.

"God works with the hands of men." The Station Master was quite clearly passing from arousal to apathy.

"Does Thomas Aquinas speak in so many words about granting dispensation from the prohibition against killing?" Grand Master Swaczyna asked.

"Yes, in so many words," Station Master Ujejski barely moved his lips. "He says that people are given dispensation from the prohibition against killing since, according to human law, it is permitted to kill people—for instance criminals or enemies."

"Absolutely right, as far as I'm concerned," threw in Commandant Jeremiah. "As far as I'm concerned, I'm for the death penalty. It will be better for more than one scoundrel if he is buried before it is too late."

"I could say," Mr. Trąba said with a somewhat forced smile, "I could say that all the arguments mentioned suit my dying intentions well. Dispensation from the Fifth Commandment suits me. Permission to kill an enemy and a criminal suits me. The existence of capital punishment suits me. Incidentally, as far as the medieval opinion on the licitness of tyrannicide is concerned—I'm speaking to you, Mr. Station Master, but you're sleeping," and indeed the Station Master's eyes were closed, and his head had fallen onto his chest, "—as far as the medieval opinion on tyrannicide is concerned, this was partially revoked by the Council of Constance. But of course we Lutherans— maybe it is better that you're sleeping, Mr. Station Master—we Lutherans don't care about either Thomas Aquinas or some council from the mists of history. We Lutherans care about Luther. And Luther— although he does not allow tyrannicide—allows punishment. 'Be ye therefore merciful, as your Father is also merciful,' he cites Scripture, but it does not follow from this, he adds, that there shouldn't be punishment at all. There must be punishment, and it is the superior authorities who are to punish. If injustices should not cease, make report about this, says Luther, to your superior authority, your father or whomever is placed over you to exercise office: it is their task to punish according to righteousness. Yes," Mr. Trąba sighed deeply, "I think it is clear to all that in the current situation, here and now, the Reformer's recommended legalism is a troublesome utopia, and it is necessary to take matters into our own hands. Gomułka's superior authority is Khrushchev, and if I wanted to abide strictly by the counsel of Doctor Martin Luther, I would have to direct my complaint against Gomułka to Khrushchev. Which is absurd."

"It's only slightly less absurd than killing Gomułka." Commandant Jeremiah persisted in his increasingly peculiar commonsense argumentation.

"No, a hundred times no," Mr. Trąba raised his voice. "I've worked the problem out theoretically without a hitch, just as I hope to hit him in the heart without a hitch. I name myself, in the name of historical righteousness, the superior authority of First Secretary Władysław Gomułka, and as the superior power I will mete out the death penalty to him."

"And thereby you ennoble him, Mr. Trąba. You will join the ranks of the great assassins of mankind, but you also add Gomułka to the ranks of the great tyrants of mankind. Doesn't that bother you?" asked Grand Master Swaczyna.

"This pains me, but unfortunately there are no ideal solutions," Mr. Trąba replied, and he turned to Father Pastor Potraffke:

"I'm terribly sorry, but whom did you have in mind? What Protestants took part in assassination attempts upon the highest power?"

"Not searching too far afield, a certain Lutheran, Bogumił Frankemberg, a locksmith from Cybulice, took part in the famous, although fortunately failed, attempt on the life of the last king of the Commonwealth."

"You are thinking of the disgraceful abduction of Stanisław August Poniatowski that ended with the retreat of the conspirators, with the exception of one who, seeing what was happening, went over to the side of the king? Do you have in mind the famous coup that ended with the rescue of our last crowned head by an accidental miller in Marymont?" Mr. Trąba was making certain he'd understood correctly.

"Your coup will end up just the same, a fiasco, everything will come to nothing, you'll wander around, you'll get lost, you'll end up, if not in a mill in Marymont, then in the police station on Marszałkowska Street, you'll get drunk as swine." Commandant Jeremiah had clearly lost what was left of his patience. "By the way, why aren't you drinking, Mr. Trąba? After all, you were supposed to be dying of drink, and for that reason you intend to commit a crime. And what do I see here? You're not drinking?"

"You go too far, Commandant." Mr. Trąba grew pale, and his hands began to shake. "Those arguments are below the belt. Moreover, in a plan of elementary logic you confuse causes with effects."

"Brothers, calm yourselves," Pastor Potraffke once again appealed for peace. "And what if," he continued in a tone of somewhat too studied conciliation, "what if you were to tie this not to the idea of real regicide, since it is indeed difficult to find an example of that in our history, but to the idea of symbolic regicide?"

"Just what do you have in mind?" Father asked.

"There are known cases of attempts not upon the person of the ruler but upon his image. For example, Prince Józef Jabłonowski, enraged at that same unfortunate Stanisław August Poniatowski, ordered a portrait of the king hung in his private dungeon, and he placed guards by that imprisoned image. Likewise the portrait of King Jan III Sobieski fell victim to an assassin's attempt. A certain nobleman, whose name I don't remember, simply hacked the likeness of the king to pieces with his saber, for which, moreover, he paid with his neck."

"Don't be angry with me, Pastor, but the idea that I should let fly from my crossbow at a photograph of Władysław Gomułka cut out of *The People's Tribune*—well that sort of idea is humiliating." Mr. Trąba's hands continued to shake, and his gaze strayed time and again in the direction of the bottles that were standing on the table.

"You must be aware," Commandant Jeremiah's tone seemed to reveal that perhaps he was slowly beginning to come to terms with the irreversible course of events, "you must be aware that, in addition to everything else, the crossbow isn't the weapon of knights but of servants. Gentlemen despise the crossbow. For example, the use by the

British of massive units armed with crossbows in the famous Battle of Crécy was recognized as dishonorable by the theological faculty of the Sorbonne, which, in itself, invalidated the result of the battle. The use of the crossbow is a foul."

"I don't intend to foul Gomułka. I intend to kill him," Mr. Trąba retorted dully. "The crossbow is the only weapon I know that can be effective at a distance of 150 to 200 yards. On the other side of Frascati Street, across from the windows of the first secretary's apartment, there stretches a small park, and precisely from that spot, from behind the cover of darkness and leafless shrubs, I intend to send forth a single, and I hope lethal, shot. I choose the crossbow because, as I have mentioned many times, I simply don't know how to use firearms. Obviously, I know perfectly well about the course of the Battle of Crécy, and I know that in Europe that weapon never enjoyed great esteem. But as always, excessive Eurocentrism is what destroys us Europeans. As some of you may know, the crossbow was invented in China, and at a time when bears were strolling back and forth across today's Frascati Street. The trigger mechanisms of Chinese crossbows were produced with the precision of a grain of rice, and their level of complication, as experts claim, is comparable to that of bullet chambers in contemporary automatic rifles. You can find breathtaking descriptions of these constructions (handmade, although on an industrial scale) in old Chinese tracts, for example in *The Art of War of Master Sun* or in *Springs and Autumns of Mr. Lu*. I have the impression that both texts stem from the times when our ancestors, who later despised the weapon as unworthy of gentlemen, were still frightening wild animals with their ghastly dialect. The Huns, who battled with the Chinese, feared the crossbow, but if, by some miracle, they came into possession of one, they were unable to assemble or copy it. They weren't even able to make use of the arrows, since they were too short for their long bows. Thus the invention and use of the crossbow is a flight of human thought and technology, a rebuff to barbarity. The fact that, one thousand years after the Chinese, servants in Europe used crossbows to set fire to barns is rather a measure of the demise, and not a manifestation of the exquisite manners, of the warriors of *Mitteleuropa*. So you see, it was no coincidence," Mr. Trąba glanced in the direction of Grand Master Swaczyna, "no coincidence at all that I chose the Chinese model, since just like the ancient Chinese, I intend to rout the Huns. Even more, I intend to kill the very leader of the Huns."

"As I said," Grand Master Swaczyna reached into his breast pocket and extracted a folded piece of office paper, "as I said, the idea of killing, whether it's a communist leader or any other sort of leader, is, in my opinion, an idea for students, but a commission remains a commission. 'The customer is our master,' as the latest slogan of socialized services proclaims. Here's the project."

Grand Master Swaczyna smoothed out the paper, and we all caught sight of a scrupulously drawn image of a beautiful object, shaded with a soft pencil, like an old illustration.

"The bed is approximately thirty, and precisely thirty-three and one half inches in length, and will be produced from beech wood, buffalo horn, and ram's tendons," Grand Master Swaczyna explained. "The inlay: little circles and rosettes of ivory. It all worked out well— I recently imported a little ivory from Kenya at a small profit. The bowstring will be of horse hair, the trigger lever of brass. Whereas for the bail, that is to say the bow, we will employ a spring from a Citroën model 1938. Only yesterday I paid a visit to one of my workshops and personally inspected the death-dealing metal. It has already been cleaned of rust and petrified mud. I can tell you all that truly murderous powers lurk in its wings glistening with olive intensity. As the man from whom I bought the spring assured me, that very Citroën model 1938 was in its time the property of the legendary murderer Mazurkiewicz. There remains the questions of shots, that is to say arrows . . ."

"One arrow will be enough," Mr. Trąba studied the details of the project carefully. "One arrow will be enough, made, as I told you, from a bicycle spoke and wooden ailerons, whereas the tip is to be made from a silver ball filed off of Mrs. Chief's souvenir sugar bowl." Mr. Trąba bowed slightly in the direction of Mother, who was sitting motionless.

"And the silver blade will pierce his bowels, and his belly, and the dirt shall come out. Poland, Poland," resounded Father Pastor Potraffke's hoarsely distorted voice.

Once again he raised up his arms, but now it might seem that he lifted on them a huge, invisible weight, and his face grew pale as paper, he panted heavily, his dark, fiery pupils fled time and again into the depths of his skull. The Pastor's Wife jumped up from her place, but neither she nor any of us, who were seized with sudden fear, knew what to do. Pastor Potraffke now raised up his arms and the weight resting on them (all the heavier for the fact that it was invisible), and now he himself rose up from his place, and apoplectic blotches began to appear on his face, which gave the impression that he was slowly returning to life and consciousness. And indeed, he lowered one hand and extracted a Bible from his jacket pocket. He opened it with a mechanical, though seemingly infallible, gesture, and with a somewhat calmer, though still sufficiently apoplectic voice, he began to speak, read, and comment:

"I ask you, beloved brothers and beloved sisters, how many years have passed since the end of the war until today, until the year of our Lord 1963? Eighteen years. Eighteen. Listen, then, to what the Book of Judges has to say: 'And the children of Israel did evil again in the sight of the Lord: and the Lord strengthened Eglon the king of Moab against Israel, because they had done evil in the sight of the Lord. So the children of Israel,' listen carefully brothers and sisters, 'the children of Israel served Eglon the king of Moab for eighteen years.' Just as we," the pastor raised up his head and immediately let it drop again, "just as we have been serving the king of the Huns for eighteen years. Scripture speaks in this passage, the Book of Judges, chapter three, verse fourteen, about precisely eighteen years of bondage: 'But when the children of Israel cried unto the Lord, the Lord raised them up a deliverer, Ehud the son of Gera, a man who did not use his right hand: and by him the children of Israel sent a present unto Eglon the king of Moab. But Ehud made him a dagger which had two edges, of a cubit length; and he did gird it under his raiment on his right thigh. And he brought the present unto Eglon king of Moab: and Eglon was a very fat man. And Ehud came unto him and put forth his left hand and took the dagger forth from his right thigh and thrust it into his belly. So that the haft also went in after the blade; and the fat closed upon the blade, so that he could not draw the dagger out of his belly; and the dirt came out.' That's right. Dirt. Poland."

Father Pastor Potraffke finished his furious, though ever quieter and ever calmer, reading from the Book of Judges, sat down heavily,

95

and cast his careful gaze with unwaning fury across everyone sitting at the table, and then he said out of the blue:

"Nothing in the world, nothing will bring me to grant you confirmation. Dirt. Dirt. Poland. Poland."

"Poland," Mr. Trąba repeated after him as if an echo.

"Poland," Grand Master Swaczyna repeated as if it were the response to a password.

"Poland, goal," said Father.

"Poland, Poland, Poland," said Mother, the Pastor's Wife, and Małgosia Snyperek.

"Poland, Poland, Poland," we began to repeat, one after another, to chant in unison "Poland, Poland," like fans sitting in the same section of a stadium.

And the choralists, who were still standing on the podium and were still singing Czech songs to the accompaniment of the missionary orchestra, finally heard our "Poland, Poland," for they finally fell silent for a moment, and not at all surprised, not even directing astounded glances in our direction, they immediately sang in Polish, with that same strong voice:

> "Time to go home, it's time. They already call us.
> The bell from the tower to devotions,
> Mother from the doorway to supper.
> They already call, it's time to go home, time."

And we had to admit, and we always admitted later, and with genuine fervor, that the the morphinistes' Czech boyfriends sang that old Polish song so skillfully that none of us heard even a hint of a foreign accent in their singing.

Chapter VII

I FELT THE ROCKING OF THE ASSASSINS' POSTAL AMBULANCE CAR AS it glided slowly along the tracks through the muddy plains. I awoke and fell asleep, again and again. I breathed in the smell of packing paper, hemp twine, and wax seals. In the darkness I saw pyramids of packages and parcels. Mr. Trąba, Father, and the postal guards sat in the middle of those pyramids. I heard the murmur of their conversations. They spoke of women: love stories, like the dark fields, stations, and lights we passed along the way, followed one after the other.

I listened to tales about women with fluent mastery of the pen, and I listened to stories about women with fluent mastery of foreign languages. I heard about romances with overworked widows and romances with lazy young ladies. I listened to complaints full of bitterness and longings full of despair. Here were the poetic landscapes of first encounters, detailed descriptions of apartments of extreme raptures, and curt sketches of the places of shameful separations. I listened to imprecations, admonitions, and aphorisms full of paradoxical wisdom about the power of women, or pamphlet-like treatises on the art of wearing a brassiere.

I listened to adventures full of arousing plot developments, but I wasn't able to distinguish the voices, to say who told which story. Even

Mr. Trąba's theatrical whisper was difficult to distinguish. I don't think Father spoke up at all. Maybe he was speaking just as I would fall off to sleep, or maybe I would fall off to sleep whenever he began to speak. I don't remember.

•

I don't remember a thousand scenes in which he took part. I don't remember him playing soccer with me in the rocky courtyard. I don't remember the gesture with which he would adjust his glasses. I don't remember outings to Buffalo Mountain during which he would teach me the names of the trees and the birds. I don't remember the way he would turn the huge sheets of the newspapers he read. I don't remember his daily return from the post office. To tell the truth, I don't really know very well what he did all those years after he took early retirement. I described the scene, but I don't really remember whether Father ran with the other men through the high Asiatic grass in the direction of the morphinistes at the edge of the glade that evening. Or whether he walked with a very quick step. Or was it perhaps the opposite? That he didn't budge from the spot?

Even today, it seems to me that although I remember every word of his unending disputes with Mr. Trąba, I don't remember certain gestures, poses, his gait. I don't remember how he sat on a chair. I remember him, but I don't see him. Or is it perhaps the opposite: I see him all the time in one and the same scene, which repeats endlessly but is over in a moment?

Could it be that, in its quotidian obtrusiveness, that one, peculiar, although characteristic, picture has forced out and obscured all the others? It goes like this: Father sits at the table in our kitchen, which is as gigantic as a Greek amphitheater. Mr. Trąba says something to him. Father gets up, walks over to the sideboard, takes out a bottle, returns, and puts it on the table. That scene, repeating itself in my memory with absolute inevitability for the hundredth, thousandth, millionth time, slowly becomes monstrous. Father's movements become more and more violent, as if they were shaped by internal spasms and resistance. The interior of the kitchen grows dark. Under the empty space an invisible fire burns. Ash falls from above. It is as if

Mr. Trąba really did command Father, throughout his whole life and a hundred times a day: get up from the table, walk over to the sideboard, take out the bottle, get up from the table, walk over to the sideboard, take out the bottle, get up from the table, walk over to the sideboard, take out the bottle.

Perhaps I don't remember anything more because, in a certain sense, I had my back turned to him my whole life. He would do something, bustle about, adjust something, rustle the newspapers, read, type at the typewriter, listen to Radio Free Europe. Perhaps he ran after me, but I, with my ruthless, perhaps even inhuman pig-headedness, went my own false and mad way.

When, after forty years, I finally looked around, I caught sight of four stools standing in the middle of our kitchen. On the stools lay the basement door, which had been removed from its hinges. On the door, dressed in his postal chief's uniform, lay Father. Mother was lighting funeral candles. Mr. Trąba stood by the window. I went up to him. For a moment we looked at the pallbearers walking through the yard. On their shoulders, the lid and bottom of the coffin looked like the wings of an airplane, crashed long ago, that had just now been found in the grass.

"I know that people always say this, and in every latitude on the globe, but the Chief looks like he's sleeping," said Mr. Trąba.

•

That very day Mother and I began to put Father's death in order, to seek out the internal logic in it, and to look for the signs of its approach in the last days of his life. With fierce meticulousness we began to gather and remind each other of the facts and circumstances that could have brought the undying order of death into play. Hour by hour, minute by minute, we reconstructed the final days and weeks of Father's life, describing precisely, attesting, emphasizing, laying out, and bringing to the surface all the seemingly accidental events, gestures, and objects in which the portent of his death might have been rooted. We collected specimens indefatigably, and, imperceptibly, our harmonious collaboration was transformed into fierce competition. I had discovered a broken shelf in the basement, while Mother, more or less at the same time, some two weeks before his death, had encountered a macabre customer in a clothing store who had tried on nothing but black things. In my opinion, the broken shelf was a clearer sign, for the oak plank had snapped as if cut by an unearthly power. The preserves had come crashing down from on high, and—what do you know?—not a single jar had broken.

The encounter in the clothing store with the woman trying on mourning clothes made a more accidental impression, but you had to admit that Mother told the story suggestively, the story of the shiver of terror that pierced her when she stood right next to this woman. She felt a cold breath coming from those black blouses, scarves, jackets, gloves, and hats, darker than all the mourning clothes in the world. And the woman herself, as tall as a basketball player, skinny, bony, with glowing sulfurous eyes—no two ways about it: she looked like death itself.

Mother also told how, exactly a week before his death—exactly a week, since he died on a Wednesday, and that was also a Wednesday—Father first saw Mr. Trąba off as far as the gate, which was strange in itself, since he did that very rarely. And he didn't return for the longest time. He walked around the garden, examined the apple and plum trees, touched an old cherry tree, bent over, as if he were picking something up from the grass, and then he dawdled about the house, until Mother got irritated that he was dawdling and dawdling—didn't that bother him, she wondered? But then he went up into the attic, down to the basement, wandered through all the rooms, rummaged about as if he were looking for something, but really he was saying goodbye, just saying goodbye to everything.

And Bryś the Man-Eater, I suddenly recalled, do you remember how Bryś the Man-Eater fled from him? That was about a month earlier, six weeks before his death. Of course, Mother said, the first signs always appear six weeks before someone's death. Commandant Jeremiah was taking Bryś on a walk. They stopped by our gate. They didn't even come inside. Mother exchanged some meaningless pleasantries about the weather with the Commandant. Bryś the Man-Eater obediently crouched by his leg. But as soon as he saw Father standing on the porch he began to howl desperately and heart-wrenchingly, and he rushed into awkward, disorderly flight. We laughed at him, that he'd completely gone off his head in his old age. The oldest dog in the world (after all, as the Commandant explained, he *is* fifty years old) has a right to stranger whims than that. We laughed at the moribund old geezer, but he knew what he was doing. He howled, and he tried so desperately to flee, as if he felt the unearthly smell of death coming from Father, as as if he saw that somebody invisible was standing next to Father, someone who strikes fear into all creation.

In silence, in complete silence, without a word, Mother showed me Father's watch, which she had taken off his wrist. The watch had stopped precisely with his last breath at 3:20. And then she showed me her watch, the hands of which had also stopped at 3:20, and then she pointed to both second-hands, both equally and identically immobilized on the 12, and then she recalled that in the last week of his life Father had gotten it into his head that he had to go to Warsaw on some urgent business. She was at wit's end. He insisted furiously, as if something had taken possession of him. Finally she was able to convince him, and he stayed home. He stayed, and he died at home. That too, after all, is a sign of God's grace, for, be that as it may, at least he didn't keel over somewhere out in the world.

And so, we reminded each other of signs, and we made signs. We investigated whether Father's death was accidental, whether it was inevitable, whether it was foreordained, or whether he was to blame for it, whether he could have avoided it, and whether he had wanted to avoid it, or whether, on the contrary, he had consciously gone to meet it. We placed question marks, and we summoned for help the watch hand, the fleeing dog, and all the objects that the deceased had touched. We attempted to penetrate the darkness. We did all that, and yet, after all, we also knew that he had long suffered serious heart problems, and that a year before he died the doctors had given him at most a year to live.

•

Ambulance. In Father and Mr. Trąba's conversations, the word "ambulance" appeared very frequently. It appeared so frequently and persistently that the game of foreseeing its constant presence was boring and sterile. "No problem for me, I'll take the ambulance," Father would say. "I'll send that by the ambulance," "The ambulance will take us there," "Everything we need can be put on the ambulance." Ambulance, ambulance, ambulance—I pondered the movement, darkness, and roundness of that word, and I sensed the smell of wax seals. Then, imperceptibly, "ambulance" disappeared from our household, perhaps it disappeared entirely from the Polish language. With all certainty, in none of the hundreds of thousands, and perhaps millions, of sentences I have read in the meantime has the word ambulance appeared. I would have noticed it without fail and with all intensity, just as right away, with Proustian, madeleine-inspired intensity, I noticed it in Father's posthumous papers. I was looking through those yellowed petitions to the Ministry of Communication and the District Office of the Post and Telecommunications. I read the dim typescripts Father had laboriously tapped out on the old English "Everest" typewriter. I read accusations and notifications of the initiation of proceedings printed on the official forms of the District Office of the Post and Telecommunications.

> Disciplinary proceedings have been initiated against you on account of your infringement of official responsibilities, whereby, while employed in the position of Chief of an Office of the Post and Telecommunications, over the course of the year 1959 you exploited your position and sent private packages containing veal by postal ambulance, and at the same time you prevailed upon the personnel to transport those packages to the addresses of certain employees of the District Office of the Post and Telecommunications.

I read findings of punishment, composed with no little stylistic virtuosity, and comprehensive justifications for the findings of punishment.

> Since the above-cited proofs confirm irrefutably the commission by the accused of the deeds mentioned in the content of the accusation, to wit: the sending of private packages containing veal by postal ambulance, and the pressure put upon the personnel of the ambulances to transport said packages, I recommend the

administration of severe disciplinary punishment. Disciplinary Spokesman for the District Office of the Post and Telecommunication, Okoński, *M.A.*

With an aching heart, my throat choking up, I deciphered barely legible copies of desperate explanatory letters and plaintive petitions. I read applications and negative replies to applications, requests and interventions and negative replies to requests and interventions. Line by line I studied that black-and-white record of Father's dialogue with a Postal Service that was as vast as nothingness.

I explain as follows: In the year 1959, in the area of Katowice, there occurred a passing, although serious, lack of meat products, above all veal. In view of this, knowing that, in the area of Wisła and its neighboring Istebna, there existed the possibility of acquiring veal, some employees of the District Office of the Post and Telecommunications in Katowice turned to me with the request that I buy meat and send it to them by the ambulance. I saw to this matter as a courtesy and without personal profit. I turn to you with the humble request for intervention in the matter of my removal from the position of Chief of the OPT and prejudicial transferal to the OPT in Cieszyn.

In reference to your letter, the District Office of the Post and Telecommunications informs you that, regarding the initiation of disciplinary action against you in the matter of the transportation by postal ambulance of private packages containing veal, the decision to transfer you remains in effect.

In view of the above, I once again ask for help and intervention. In view of my illness, the commute to work of nearly three hours in each direction is unusually onerous, and in winter practically impossible.

Regarding your letter concerning the matter of the prejudicial transferal, a final answer will be conveyed to you at a later date.

103

This is to inform you that your request concerning the granting of a two-month unpaid leave is postponed until the disciplinary hearing has taken place.

Regarding the initiation of disciplinary proceedings against me in the matter of transporting private packages containing veal by postal ambulance, I humbly request to be informed what stage my case has now reached. Eight months have already passed since the initiation of proceedings.

The Secretariat of the Ministry informs you that the disciplinary hearing against you concerning allegations by the Spokesman for Disciplinary Matters in the matter of your transportation by postal ambulance of private packages containing veal will be conducted by the Disciplinary Commission at the District Office of the Post and Telecommunications in Cracow. Attached is a finding for punishment as well as a list of the members of the full adjudicating assembly. You are informed herewith that the appointed time for the hearing has been set for 27 July of the current year at nine o'clock A.M. The hearing will take place in the auditorium of the Trade Union of Communications Employees in Cracow, Librowszczyzna Street 1. You are required to appear at the hearing in person.

Adjudication by the Disciplinary Commission of the District Office of the Post and Telecommunications in Cracow. The object of the adjudication: accused . . . born . . . employed . . . previously unpunished disciplinarily, accused of infringement of official duties committed by exploiting his position as the Chief of the Office of the Post and Telecommunications, that, using employees subordinate to himself, he did transport by postal ambulance private packages containing veal to the addresses of certain employees of the District Office of the Post and Telecommunications, is, after the conclusion of an oral hearing, declared innocent and exonerated of the above-mentioned charges. The citizen is declared innocent on account of lack of evidence of official transgression in the deeds charged against him.

•

"You were debased by Moscow, Chief, debased through and through, and you will forgive me if I don't share your premature joy." Mr. Trąba seemed absolutely immune to Father's enthusiasm that day.

"From the beginning I knew that justice would be done," Father triumphed, "from the very beginning. And when I learned that Cracow had been designated as the place of the hearing, I no longer had a hint of fear or doubt. Cracow is Cracow! There were only prewar chiefs, gentleman chiefs, on the board of the adjudicating commission." Father choked on his own saliva. "Chief Czyż, Chief Holeksa, Chief Kozłowski, every inch the gentlemen, suits, good manners, broad horizons. . ."

"I see that you, Chief, have developed a taste for disciplinary hearings," Mr. Trąba allowed himself an almost openly contemptuous tone.

"If you only knew, Mr. Trąba, if you only knew. It is worth meeting people like Chief Kozłowski under any circumstance." Father swaggered at the table and sought, however unsuccessfully, to pose like a victorious sailor who had just returned from a dangerous expedition.

I well remember Father's return, not simply declared innocent and exonerated, but quite triumphant. I remember not only the words, but also the gestures, for that day abounded in particularly frequent risings from the table, walks over to the sideboard, and removals from it of successive, very successive, bottles.

"What fairytales are you trying to tell me, Chief? You can't have become that Bolshevized! I understand that you spent some time in Russky bondage and that you have a right to certain complexes, but—by a billion barrels of beer—you aren't a young poet who needs to base his entire life on traumatic events! The very fact that a proceeding was initiated against you was a crime."

"To tell the truth, what I did wasn't entirely in order." Father now attempted to speak in a sort of boldly canny manner.

"Chief, don't fall prey to any illusions, and don't make yourself into some sort of capo of the meat mafia who not only ran afoul of the organs of justice but even hoodwinked them. What did you do? You did nothing. Once a week you sent a little bit of veal by train so that your so-called friends wouldn't croak from hunger. That's what you did. And for that you were debased."

"I was declared innocent, and exonerated," Father answered with puffed up dignity.

"Do you know, Chief, what's the most terrible thing about Moscow? The most terrible thing is the fact that, in her omnipotence, Moscow wishes to imitate God, that it is the Antichrist."

"You exaggerate, Mr. Trąba, as usual you exaggerate." Sunk in an absolute state of bliss, intoxicated with his evanescent relief, and, quite simply, already pretty well potted, Father wouldn't hear any arguments. He didn't realize that all of Mr. Trąba's admonitions and ominous suppositions would be fulfilled to the letter, that they had already begun to come true.

"Just as almighty God works with the hands of his servants, the people, so Moscow debased you with the hands of its servants, the employees of the District Office of the Post and Telecommunications. They declared you innocent, but all the same, you won't return to your position, or to your office. You will continue to commute for now in rain, heat, and stormy weather to far-away Cieszyn. You will lose your health. You will hand over generous bribes in an attempt to obtain the sick leave that is coming to you. In your apparently innocent, but in reality endless degradation, you will continue to experience constant humiliations. You will continue to write and to send petitions:

> "'In connection with the fact that I have been declared innocent of the charge that, in transporting packages containing veal by ambulance, I had infringed upon my official duties, I humbly ask for transferal, return, and annulment.'

"And the Antichrist will continue to respond to you by the hands of his secretaries:

> "'In answer to your question, you are hereby informed that your petition was not accompanied by the appropriate attestations and attachments . . . will be examined at a later date . . . was settled negatively.'

"Yes, that's how it will be, that's how it will be, Chief. Too bad I can't take your picture, because if you could take a look tomorrow at a daguerrotype of your face, lit up as it is with childish happiness, you would grasp that three months outside of Moscow in Serpukhov is a trifle in comparison with true bondage."

Mr. Trąba looked for a moment at Father's irregularly nodding head (it was flying through golden spaces), and he added in a jauntier tone:

"And yet, as they say, there isn't anything so bad that it couldn't get worse. When you come to your senses, when you finally make a hard landing on earth, when you grasp that the nightmare hasn't ended, rather that it has taken on definiteness, this will give you strength. You will grow manly in your disaster. You will become a little bitter. You will become a little cynical. Perhaps even a note of gallows' humor will arise in your noble nature. Don't be angry, but, from my point of view, this will be better. You would become a more interesting disputational partner, more inclined to resistance. Yes, Chief, we will chat, we will drink a little, we will philosophize. We will be like the heroes of a novel that has come unglued. We will be like literary figures that, instead of acting lazily though comprehensively, will talk over our fates from all sides. But that, too, only for a time. For a time, Chief. For a time, since the hour of our deed will also ring forth."

•

In addition to the smell of packing paper, hemp twine, and wax seals, perhaps there still smoldered in the rocking ambulance the smell of calves' blood. But I didn't smell it; I didn't know the necessary details at the time. If the specter of any sort of blood flitted through my half-conscious head at all, it was quite certainly the blood of Władysław Gomułka, which we were supposed to shed in less than twenty-four hours. I continually awoke and fell asleep, and I listened to the voices of the men as they told the story of one love-affair after another.

"And in that way I came to the conclusion," someone's dark, subdued voice was finishing a sad, or perhaps a happy, story, "in that way I came to the conclusion that the only thing I demand from a woman is that she wear a brassiere with style. That's right. I demand style in the wearing of a brassiere. Nothing else."

"A proper demand," a second subdued voice added to the discussion, "a proper demand. After all, this is something no man can do."

Suppressed giggles resounded, glasses clinked delicately, and the train slowed down.

"I had the misfortune," someone had clearly succumbed to the spell of Mr. Trąba's narcotic manner of speaking, although this was certainly not him; the unfamiliar half-whisper sounded too youthful and unstable, "I had the misfortune to start a romance, once upon a time, with a woman with fluent mastery of the pen. I was never keen about people who had fluent mastery of the pen, but my knowledge about the fact that there existed women who had fluent mastery of the pen was highly theoretical. In any event, I had never met a writing woman, to say nothing of one who wrote so ecstatically, so greedily, and—I'm aware that this sounds risqué—who wrote in every situation. She buried me under piles of letters and letterlets, little slips of paper, hundreds of confessions, thousands of notes, occasional poems, and accidental short stories, inspired descriptions of what she did yesterday, and what she would do today. Everywhere I came upon sheets of paper covered with her sprawling handwriting and folded in her characteristically refined manner. Every time I reached into my pocket, I came upon some text. I constantly removed them, and I constantly found them. I removed them not only because I was quite simply afraid that they would fall into my wife's hands, which were not itching, or rather *were itching*, to kill me—that too; but this woman with fluent mastery of the pen produced such quantities of records that the quantity itself was the main problem. One way or another, I had to reduce their monstrous number. I didn't have any doubt that sooner or later one of these scraps, which were lying about everywhere and flying out from every corner, would fall into my wife's hands. And that is just what happened. To tell the truth, it happened many times. Luckily, a significant portion of the writings of the woman with fluent mastery of the pen were hermetic writings, and, thanks to happy coincidences, on each occasion my wife came upon statements that were unclear, basically incomprehensible. Nonetheless she always attentively unfolded and flattened out the little notes that she found everywhere, put on her glasses, and read. Or rather, she studied them carefully. And then, she would raise her glance and look at me with a sympathy that was full of pain, as if she were aware what sort of forced labor there is in a romance with a graphomaniac, with such a pampered soul that is compelled to pour out all—that's right—*all* her emotions onto paper. But the woman with fluent mastery of the pen was not a graphomaniac. This thirty-year-old, who measured 40-24-38 . . ."

"Our congratulations," someone's voice spoke up, and then a round of applause resounded behind the wall of packages and parcels that separated me from the narrators and listeners.

"I thank you from the bottom of my heart," the narrator clearly bowed to his listeners, who had rewarded him with bravos. "So you see, this dusky thirty-year-old had literary talent, without a doubt, and she also had the sometimes troublesome awareness of her talent. Just imagine, she even offered me her shopping lists, since she believed that she had worked out those litanies wittily and deftly from the literary point of view. And—would you believe it?—they *were* worked out wittily and deftly. She wrote quickly, without reflection, and almost every one of her texts merited attention." I heard a delicate rustling. "Every one of her texts. Even a shopping list. Even a little note left at the head of my bed. Listen, gentlemen. I quote:

"'It's 9:00 in the morning. Monday. 10 July (1961). I'm going out. You, dear M., try not to do that, i.e., don't go out. I'll return. I kiss you, in spite of the fact that my kiss has to penetrate the yellowish cloud that shrouds your unfortunate body. Herbal liqueurs at this hour (I remind you—it's 9:00 in the morning) clearly change one's state of concentration. They have transformed themselves into a yellow cloud; by the time of my return, may it have moved somewhere else. Let it lower over any other district of our capital bourg, over Żoliborz or over Saska Kępa. Let it move in the direction of Upper Silesia, or in the direction of the Land of the Thousand Lakes. Let it cross the borders of our Piast State and lower over one or the other of the oppressed Baltic republics. Let it flow further and stop over the Baikonur Cosmodrome, from which Yuri Gagarin blasted off, or over the little village of Smetovka, near which he landed. Let it lower with its mournful shade over the state of Idaho in order to honor the suicidal death of Ernest Hemingway. Let the yellow cloud with the unclear outlines of your unconscious body lower wherever. Let it even lower over the fighting Congo. I wouldn't wish, dear M., to excite you too much, but I want you to put it you know where. All I care about is that you not drink anything more. Take a bath. Eat something. I'll be back at 7:00 P.M. Your F . . .'

"You'll have to agree . . ."

"Indeed," this time I didn't have a shadow of a doubt: this was Mr. Trąba's whisper, "indeed, as far as the literary genre is concerned, which we might casually term the 'personal note,' there is a certain magisterial quality, but was there anything more? Did the undoubted, although—how to put it?—rather specialized, talent of your friend develop somehow further?"

"I don't know. I lost sight of her. One day one of her notes fell into my wife's hands that were itching to kill me, and, unfortunately, this time it wasn't a hermetic note, either in content or in form. To tell the truth, it was a text that was glaring in its ostentatious effusiveness. For obvious reasons I remember every word:

> "'You won't believe it,' wrote my mistress with fluent mastery of the pen, 'you won't believe it, but I like everything, I like it everywhere. I like it when you are delicate, and I like it when you are brutal. I like it when you do it in a flash, and I like it when you do it for a long time. As the poet says, all the gates to my body open before you with identical eagerness. I like the smell of your sweat, and I like the smell of your cologne. I like pain, and I like the lack of pain. And besides that, I don't know whether you know, my Big Bear, what beautiful eyes you have.'"

A moment of silence fell. The train rumbled. There was something unusual in the fact that I heard each word of the more and more shamefaced whispers in spite of the constant rumbling.

"And how did your esteemed spouse react?"

"She stamped her foot."

"Yes, that usually suffices," said Mr. Trąba with distinct satisfaction, and he continued in a subdued voice. "I fear that your talented friend wasn't conscious of her talent after all, because, in my opinion, women aren't conscious of their talents in general. I'll say more: they aren't even conscious of the talent of their bodies. Gentlemen! I saw the most beautiful woman in the world in Cracow on Wiślna Street. She stood on the curb. She was looking in the direction of the Market Square, and under her gaze the lights of the square were going out. I won't describe the details, since this is not about entrancing, absolutely entrancing, corporality, but rather about a fundamental psychological question. In any case, she had an exceedingly daring shape. Gentlemen, restrain your ill-timed giggles. I want you to understand me well. Obviously, having the choice between shape and lack of shape, on the whole, in the course of my sufficiently long life, I have regularly chosen shape. But for shape alone to be the goal of the assault—never, no, not ever. In this regard, I was always a hunter of integrality per se. And besides, you gentlemen certainly know at least this much: granted, the lack of shape doesn't give any guarantees, but it also doesn't have to be an obstacle to achieving the greatest raptures. Finally, however many times I recall my unfortunate ward Emilia, my most dramatic moment of non-fulfillment (and I recall her more and more often), every time I come to the conclusion that Emilia and I would have achieved everything and reached everywhere. Yes, I'm absolutely certain that if it hadn't been for my lack of magnanimity, Emilia and I would have climbed the amorous summits . . . I'm absolutely certain of this, but, after all, the shapes of my ward Emilia, God rest her soul, were—at least from the point of view of elementary spacial categories—an absolute disaster . . . But here you have it—the absolute summit, wrapped in supple whites, stands on the curb on Wiślna Street, stands on the curb in front of a sports shoe store, stands and strains her eyes looking for someone. She waits. She doesn't while away the time of expectation by, for example, looking at the display in the sports shoe store—she doesn't examine the world while she waits. No. She waits. Now is her time for waiting. And she doesn't need to examine the world any more, because she knows everything about the world. Her world has been put in order. Everything in her world has its time, and now is the time for waiting. She has lots of things to do, and now, between one thing and another . . . she waits. Gentlemen, I sense that I'm not expressing myself clearly: it's that this absolute incarnation of carnal perfection had no right to have any non-carnal things to do; and yet, with feminine duplicity, she made it clear that she *had* such things to do. She succumbed to the female delusion that, since the problem of the form of her body had been solved perfectly, all the problems in the world that that body may have had also had been solved perfectly. Gentlemen, she was the most beautiful woman in the world, and because of this she thought that life was logical. Men who passed her took leave of their senses at the sight of this sex goddess, while she unsuccessfully pretended to be higher than her own body.

"Since she herself paid no attention—she made it clear that she paid no attention—to her own body, which was perfect, she certainly couldn't, it is clear, pay attention to other bodies that were, after all, less perfect. How in the world could someone so absolute and steeped in her own perfection bother herself with the imperfect corpuses of others—who were imperfect because they exhibited their interest in her, because of their own physiological effusiveness toward her? In that far-reaching manner, delusion in pretended indifference toward her own body condemned her to indifference toward the world. In short, in that masterpiece of tail there was nothing but sex, while she made it clear that there was everything in her *but* sex . . ."

"That's the basis of their power over us," someone said after a moment full of piercing bitterness.

"As for me, I like women's power." I immediately sensed that the greatest joker, jester, and rogue among the guards was now speaking. That's what I thought, and I wasn't mistaken. "As for me, I like women's power, because I like the kind of power you can make a fool of."

And once again, suppressed laughs and giggles resounded, glasses clinked delicately, and the train again slowed down.

"And I was once with an overworked widow with three children," said someone with a trembling voice who seemed prone to tears. "And I was once with an overworked widow with three children," he repeated once more, perhaps he repeated it for the nth time, in spite of the inaudible murmurs of disbelief, which, although they were inaudible, nonetheless must have given him strength, for he finally cast himself desperately into the whirlwind of narration.

"Yes. I was with an overworked widow. Although she was a widow, she had no financial difficulties. I think that you could even call her a rich widow. Her deceased husband—what he died of, I don't know, she never wanted to talk about it—her deceased husband quite clearly had left her a considerable estate and income. The widow drowned out her widowhood with innumerable duties and obligations, as well as with a certain excessive zeal in performing everyday tasks. It always seemed to me that she cooked broth a little bit 'more,' that she vacuumed the rug a little bit 'more,' that she ironed a blouse a little bit 'more.' She took care of her three half-orphaned children especially fiercely—that is to say, with unusually fierce motherhood. She brought up all three of them in a perfectionist manner in the general sense, but each of these brats, whom I hated intensely, also had their own specialization, which their mother had imposed upon them. The youngest girl took ballet lessons, the middle one played the piano, and the youngest boy learned foreign languages. Obviously, my overworked widow closely supervised each of these educations, and she supervised them in the rapacious manner so typical of her that I got the impression that it was she herself who practiced the ballet, played the piano, and learned foreign languages. Moreover, in a certain sense that's how it was: she did indeed practice, play, and learn. You understand, gentlemen, these were all very difficult things: her excessive zeal in performing every-day tasks was difficult, her widowhood was difficult, her cult of her deceased husband was difficult (for example, I asked her what time it was, and she said that the deceased's Delbana was still going and that it hadn't yet needed any winding), the presence of her children was difficult, her wide ranging interests were difficult. I would say that her most painful mania was framing. That's right. Framing. My overworked widow had a pathologically extensive palette of interests, and in addition a considerable portion of that palette was enclosed, literally and metaphorically, in frames. What was it about? Trivially simple things. For example, my overworked widow was a weekend painter, and, in the most ordinary manner in the world, she would mount her works, paintings, and drawings in frames and hang them on the wall. She took photographs (she had several cameras—one for black-and-white pictures, one for color pictures, one for shiny pictures, and a different one for matte pictures), and she would mount the photographs she took in frames and hang them on the wall. She would buy old etchings in antique shops, mount them in frames, and hang them on the wall. She would compose interesting flower arrangements (she was an ardent tourist, and she often took trips out of town), which she would subsequently dry, mount in frames, and hang on the wall . . ."

A sudden silence fell. Perhaps I had suddenly fallen into the black abyss of sleep. Perhaps the poor devil had stopped talking, had lost the thread, smitten with incomprehensible pain. Probably both occurred. I must have fallen asleep for a moment, but the ill-starred guard, the lover of the overworked widow with the three children, wasn't in any state to continue his terrible story.

"And then, and then?" I was awakened by slow and drowsy questions. "Well? And then? What happened then? What happened with her later? What's next?"

"Nothing. There wasn't anything. There wasn't anything next." His voice, which sounded prone to tears at the beginning of the story, now became unusually solemn and dignified. "There wasn't anything next. When I realized that I too was one of her fiercely performed duties, which, moreover, she would most prefer to mount in a frame, I felt humiliated, and I left."

Someone said:

"It won't be long now. You can see the Palace of Culture."

"You can't see anything yet. It's still dark. We have almost a whole hour to go," said someone else, who yawned terribly and fell asleep. And this time, toward the end of the journey, I fell into a deep sleep, like a man sleeping for eternity in a Dutch painting, or like an apparatchik of sleep. And then, when I awoke, I heard Father's voice, or perhaps it was still in my sleep that I heard Father's whisper, as he told the story of the man who was particularly excited by women who spoke foreign languages. Father made up stories as if he were possessed, narrated about this man as if he were talking about himself. He invented and lied fantastically. This didn't surprise me either asleep or awake. In the dark-blue depths of the postal ambulance, gliding slowly through the muddy plains, all of them invented things. After all, the story about the woman with fluent mastery of the pen was invented and entirely fictitious, and so was the one about the beauty standing on the curb on Wiślna Street, and even the one who told the story about the deadly, overworked widow with the three children made everything up. The invention of stories about oneself is the duty and irresistible temptation of the true man. The made-up story is the song of his life and death. The story of the loser, the invented story of the loser, is the sign of the winner.

"I don't know any foreign languages," Father's voice said in the darkness. "I don't speak languages, and maybe that is why I want to be—not so much exclusively as especially—with women who speak languages. But I also wish to state most emphatically that there wasn't any simple equation here; the more the better: one language—good; two languages—very good; three languages—very, and I mean *very*, exciting; and with a polyglot you have a genuine orgy. No. Unbridled symmetry arouses my resistance. I prefer restrained symmetry. One language and one woman were enough for me. After all, and finally, there is one woman," Father lied to the very faces of the guards and Mr. Trąba, although they were plunged in darkness.

And he continued his story about some completely made-up love of his who spoke dazzling French. Supposedly Father's nonexistent mistress especially liked to speak indecent sentences in French, for example: *Fouts-moi à mort. Et puis ecris sur ma tombe que j'ai pris mon pied*, she would tenderly whisper in his ear. With odd relish, that dark-haired Romanist supposedly also repeated, time and again, three words that sounded like a magic spell: *mille, villes, tranquilles, mille, villes, tranquilles*, she supposedly said time and again, and tens of times, in every situation.

"I loved her," Father lied. "We wanted to flee together to the ends of the earth. We imagined that some day, some sweltering year, we would drive with all we possessed into a city full of ginger-haired dogs, grimy children, and mysterious women wrapped in veils and turbans (with whom, after several years—such is life, gentlemen—I would doubtless betray her), and an outdoor festival, *Mille villes tranquilles*, would be in progress there. She will speak with rapture, with amazement, and we will live in a house with a view of the ocean, or with a view of meadows, or with a view of a girls' dormitory, and we will live there forever, and every night we will dream of a thousand white architectural constructions, a thousand downtown commons, a thousand sleeping streetcar sheds, and a thousand rivers crossing downtowns that are as crusty and dark as rye bread."

Everything in Father's story was invented, even the dreams were invented, which isn't so bad—dreams are always invented. But he lied even at the very beginning of this imagined romance. He even lied when he said that he didn't speak any languages. Father already knew French before the war. In those unfortunate papers he left behind, in addition to Petitions, Appeals, Pleas, Verdicts, and Accusations, there is also his Postal Practicant's Certificate, which is brittle and yellow like his buried bones: 4 May 1933, having passed the examination before the Commission of the Head Office of the Post and Telegraphs in Katowice, he received the following grades: Postal Transport—good; Postal Service—good; Bookkeeping Regulations—good; French, Speaking and Writing—very good. *Mille. Villes. Tranquilles.*

Chapter VIII

"ALL THE SAME," MR. TRĄBA SAID, "WE HAVE TO KILL HIM AND GO back home. The holidays are coming in a month."

A light rain was falling. The sky over Warsaw brightened. The first snows were lurking in the heavens. My head was adorned with a colorful headdress. I labored under the weight of the crossbow. I had a Finnish knife in my belt. On my breast sparkled a plastic sheriff's star. We wandered past prospect after prospect, we went from one end of Marszałkowska to the other, Nowy Świat, Aleje Jerozolimskie, we rode up to the top floor of the Palace of Culture. And not a soul looked at us even once.

"I hadn't realized the extent of the slavery. It's different at home in Silesia, after all." Mr. Trąba didn't bother to hide his distaste.

The tension rose. What I saw as the fiasco of our operation drew near with giant steps.

"The innocent child disguised as an Indian, and only roughly disguised at that," Mr. Trąba patted me on the headdress, "this innocent child, even this innocent child arouses fear. Why, Jerzyk looks like a colorful magic bird, like a firebird that has flown out of the pages of a fairytale onto the grey streets of this wolfish city—people should be spellbound. And here you have the opposite. Instead of slowing down, passersby speed up. Instead of casting friendly smiles, they become gloomy. Instead of nodding their heads amicably, they turn away with repugnance."

"What a hypocrite you are, Mr. Trąba. And it's likely you're entirely wrong in your social diagnosis." Father was peculiarly relaxed. "Why, this innocent child is taking part in the penultimate phase of an assassination attempt on the life of a Communist satrap, and perhaps our nation senses this with its characteristic historical intuition . . ."

"Chief!" Mr. Trąba cast a withering glance at Father. "I call you to order. Please adhere to the official version of events, even in your thoughts. After all, it's clear that in this city not only the walls have ears; this city is one giant ear . . ."

"Once again, you are guilty of moral incaution," Father laughed, "moral incaution plus desecration. Warsaw isn't a city of snitches. Warsaw is a city of heroes."

"A city of heroes has to be, at the same time, a city of informers," Mr. Trąba impatiently waved Father off. "And besides, you know, Chief, that if it were indeed as you say, that is, if our nation indeed sensed our intent with its characteristic historical intuition, it would certainly join us . . ."

"It doesn't join us. On the contrary, it scurries away, because it also senses the grotesque nature of the entire undertaking . . ."

"The grotesque doesn't exclude the spilling of blood," Mr. Trąba venomously measured out maxim after maxim. "The grotesque doesn't exclude death, the grotesque doesn't exclude shooting Władysław Gomułka with an arrow from a Chinese crossbow. On the contrary: it is precisely the grotesque that offers such a chance for reality in its entire fullness. The nation knows this . . ."

"The nation knows this from childhood, Mr. Trąba." It seemed for a moment that Father was seized by a sudden and fundamental rage, but his good humor didn't abandon him. "The nation learns, by heart, from childhood 'Get away from me! I am the murderer of tsars!' and similar thoroughly grotesque hogwash. 'It's time for me to kill . . . someone holds me by a hair.' Or even better:

'Pale, silent phantoms, weak of heart,
Like a hundred-eyed peacock sentry

118

They watch the door behind which lies
The sleeping Tsar in his bedroom . . .
Tell me, do you want to know
The color of his blood? . . .'"

"I agree with you, Chief, that, as far as our Romantics were concerned—well, that was, for the most part, a gang of hundred-eyed peacocks, which is to say unpunished graphomaniacs endowed with the useless art of rhyme. I exclude Adam Mickiewicz, of course. But let's not go too deeply into literature, it always condemns one to intellectual sterility. I want to ask you about something else." Mr. Trąba was terribly anxious. "Just why are you in such good spirits?"

"I like to travel," replied Father. "In fact, I'm in a pretty decent mood because I like to travel. Traveling soothes me. That's in the first place. And in the second place—don't be angry, Mr. Trąba—but in the second place, I'm in a good mood because I am awaiting the inexorably approaching moment when we finally throw in the towel. Strictly speaking, I'm waiting for the moment when you finally rip the Red Army flask out of your breast pocket, the one that you've been warming there from the beginning, take a healthy snort, treat me to a sip, and maybe Jerzyk too, and then all of us, relaxed, will set off for the mythical Kameralna bar, for example, in order to have a small banquet before the return trip."

"I don't feel like moving my head, so allow me once again to limit myself to waving it off." Mr. Trąba raised his arm and executed the elegant gesture of negation with nothing but his hand. "There's no turning back, Chief," he said with a voice that was horrifying, because it was absolutely credible in its helplessness. "There's no turning back, and as you know there's only one penalty for desertion. I hope Mrs. Chief didn't file the little ball off of the souvenir sugar bowl, and Grand Master Swaczyna's people didn't use their lathe to make of it a death-dealing dart, just so that I will now have to sink that piece of silver into your skeptical brain."

Father silently observed Mr. Trąba. For a moment, perhaps, he still wondered whether there were some way to turn everything into a joke. I began to feel afraid. Terror, true terror, came upon me. A tallowy half-moon rose in the empty prospect of Nowy Świat Street. As usual in those situations, I sought solace in guessing what was about to be said. I concentrated and strained, and I came to the conclusion that Father would remain silent for the time being, and that Mr. Trąba would soon say: "a cream pastry, and that's all there is to it."

Rain was falling harder and harder, and it seemed that not only the passersby, but even the architecture was scurrying away before us. Some sort of houses ran along on both sides, but almost nothing was visible. It was as if we were walking along some barely marked road through the rainy plains.

"And since we are talking about the esteemed Mrs. Chief, I remind you that we promised to dispatch a postcard. True, my bosom buddy from my student days, the most reverend Father Bishop, sends her postcards from around the world, but Warsaw is quite clearly missing from the collection." Mr. Trąba squinted and looked, in vain, for a human dwelling in the absolute emptiness. He breathed in, searching for the smell of chimney smoke with his nostrils.

·

Indeed, the bishop did send postcards from around the world. Mostly he wrote from mythical lands in which there were only Protestants. From the panoramas I composed complete images of Stockholm, Copenhagen, and Helsinki. I knew the most secret corners of Geneva, corners that were unknown even to the native Swiss, by heart. If need be, I could check the time on the famous *l'horloge fleurie*. The water-hewn shape of the fantastic fountain on the shores of Lake Geneva had already bored me to death. Just like the Swiss stamps with their monumental Helvetia, Helvetia, Helvetia.

Mother didn't allow me to unglue the stamps. To tell the truth, she didn't like it when anyone touched the cards from the bishop. I got the impression that she didn't even much like it when anyone *looked* at them. It often seemed that our very glances contained some sort of venomous, damaging powers. Once, Christ Almighty, I just couldn't resist the temptation and unglued three stamps—they were as dazzling as the Pastor's Wife's complexion—from the postcard the bishop had sent from Tanzania! I couldn't resist. I had to succumb. The skies on each of those stamps had a different color. On the first, negro shepherds tended cattle in grassy valleys, and the sky over them was orange. On the second, negro fishermen pulled nets full of fish out of the sea, and the sky over them was green. On the third, negro lumberjacks worked in the jungle, and dark-blue clouds floated just above their frizzy heads. I steamed those stamps loose. The bishop's writing—he always wrote with a fountain pen—became blurred. All you could read was the sentence: "Yesterday I preached a sermon to a congregation that was as black as coal." Mother cried. And then she hid the card I had mutilated somewhere. (She re-glued the stamps of the three skies with vegetable glue.)

I used to sneak in when she was away and open the chest. I would take out the little box—it smelled of rose oil and had once held Swiss Toblerone chocolates—in which she kept the postcards. I surveyed state after state, city after city—Edinburgh, Nairobi, Berlin, Athens, Amsterdam, Helsinki, America, England, Bulgaria, Sweden, Denmark. Tanzania was nowhere to be found. I would rummage through all the nooks of the chest. I soaked up the rose oil like a sponge. I even reached sacrilegiously into the pocket of her Sunday jacket. I opened her holiday purse. I surveyed page after page of *Protestant Homiletics*, *Crumbs from the Lord's Table*, and other of the bishop's writings—but the card with the three cloud-capped stamps had disappeared for all eternity.

•

From behind streams of rain loomed a *Ruch* kiosk filled with good things. The kiosk owner, with an unusually inhospitable facial expression, was the first person in this city who finally examined me attentively. To tell the truth, he didn't let me out of his sight. He stared at me hatefully. Father bought *The People's Tribune* and *The Catholic Weekly*. Mr. Trąba pondered which view of the Palace of Culture to choose. The kiosk owner stuck his head through the little window and shouted in an attack of insane fury:

"Carolers! St. Nicholases! Horned Beasts! People, the holidays aren't until next month, and here they are already going about caroling! Hoofed devils! Winged angels!"

I was certain that Mr. Trąba would silence him with some world-class riposte, that he would extinguish the old fart with one well-aimed phrase, but suddenly Mr. Trąba's hands started shaking. He was barely able to pay, barely able to hold the postcard in his hands. We walked off a few steps. You could still hear the sensational shouting of the kiosk owner. The rain lashed with redoubled force.

"You're absolutely right, Chief." Mr. Trąba, as pale as death, breathed heavily. He held himself up with his open palm on his heart. Or perhaps he was touching the protuberance, right at the height of his heart, that you could see through his autumn coat. In any case, one way or the other, he was propping himself up. "You're absolutely right. Crises come. Doubts grow. The closer the hour of execution, the greater my hunger for alcohol. You're absolutely right, and you foresaw all this well. The matter is, however, that I also foresaw this. Drinking, true drinking in anticipation of death, is an intensive course in self-knowledge, and I would truly be a pathetic fool if I hadn't taken into account the following inevitable eventuality: that my shattered nervous system would go into complete disarray a few hours before the event and demand elemental consolation. And so, I repeat, that unforeseeable—although otherwise absolutely foreseeable—circumstance was carefully considered in my plans. Gentlemen, don't look at me in such a panicked way. Talking soothes me. I haven't gone completely mad at the last moment. Talking soothes me, and what is more, since I feel the irresistible desire to have a drink, I intend to assuage that desire by discoursing about drinking. Like it or not, you, Chief, and you, Jerzyk, will spend this afternoon listening to my comprehensive, definitive, and testamentary lecture on the artistry of form and the tragedy of content that is the art of drinking. And you will forgive me, gentlemen, but, in spite of the circumstances, I won't invite you for this purpose to the mythical restaurant Kameralna. I invite you instead to the most exquisite, that's right, the most exquisite confectioner's shop in Eastern Europe. My treat. We're near, it's just two steps from here."

And in a few minutes we crossed the threshold of the most exquisite confectioner's shop in Eastern Europe, and we left our wet raincoats and the Chinese crossbow and arrow in the coat check room (the distinguished coat check attendant didn't even bat an eyelid), and we sat down at a little table in a cozy bay window, and the most beautiful waitress in Eastern Europe, perhaps the most beautiful waitress in the world, brought us coffee, lemon squash, and cream pastries time and again, right up until the evening.

If I say that since that afternoon, since that rainy afternoon, when we whiled away the final hours before killing Gomułka by consuming monstrous quantities of cream pastries, washing it down with coffee and lemon squash, in short, if I say that from that time, my organism harbors a sort of animosity toward cream pastries, if I say this—it won't be a surprise. And so, I will say this: in spite of the fact that I am a greedy glutton for every kind of gumdrop, in spite of the fact that I can't imagine an evening without a bar of milk chocolate, in spite of the fact that, for a middle-aged person, I nourish an excessive cult of the sweet, in spite of the fact that, for a man who, with the fierce shamelessness of the forty-something, now, in the middle of the nineties, still chases after angels who have been freed from the Muscovite yoke, in spite of the fact that I am able, with simply unmanly greediness, to gorge on sweets of every shape and color—to this day I won't touch a cream pastry.

Mr. Trąba placed the postcard with the view of the Palace of Culture on the tablecloth. He pulled an ink pencil out of his breast pocket, and, internally tense and externally trembling, he attempted to write the address with his dithering hand.

"Did you see the waitress?" Father asked. "A real *cul du siècle*. Just look at her neck. You'll feel better right away. One hunger should be cancelled out with another."

"For the moment I can't even look. For the moment I don't even know how to see. The swallows, the barn swallows are flitting about me like mad." Mr. Trąba was the embodiment of black despair. "I must at least apply an energy blockade. Praise God, she's coming . . ."

Dressed in a black skirt and a white blouse, the most beautiful waitress in the world approached from the depths of a dark hall that smelled of powdered sugar. When she placed the cream pastries (three of them) before Mr. Trąba, he immediately gobbled them down, one after the other. Those were gargantuan moments, since, unaware of his panicky movements, he smashed the pastries with his fingers. Whipped cream flowed down his chin, crumbs were falling every-where, but I have to admit that the more he ate, the faster the black flames of death in his eyes burned out, and after the last, largish bite, they went out completely.

"Better," said Mr. Trąba, "significantly better. An energy blockade is only a provisional solution, but at least it's some sort of solution."

Then he wiped his mouth with a checkered handkerchief, shook off the crumbs, licked the ink pencil, and began to write. And as he wrote he sounded out what he wrote:

"Esteemed and dear Mrs. Chief. We arrived, thanks be to God, in good form. In a few hours we will do what we must do, and what the Chief still doesn't believe we will do. I hope that everything will go according to plan, and that what must happen will finally happen. I will then flee, but the Chief will be apprehended and shackled and locked up in an underground cell for many long years. Then, dearest Mrs. Chief, we can finally link our fates. The Chief, on the other hand, will have an opportunity to cure his incurable skepticism and to be forcibly convinced that what is isn't fiction but truth. Jerzyk is completely safe and has a good appetite. We will tell you about all our other impressions, of which there are a great many, after our return . . ."

"Mr. Trąba, Mr. Trąba," Father smiled sourly, "the Fatherland is in need. In a few hours we are supposed to kill Moscow's vice-regent with our own hands, and you've got romance on your mind . . ."

"Not romance, but love of life. Please finally be convinced that I don't operate with literary constructions, but with existential phenomena."

"Here's an existential phenomenon for you." Father summoned the most beautiful waitress in the world, and craftily—with a quiet voice, so that she would have to bend over them—he ordered the next round of cream pastries.

"Verily, you were right." Mr. Trąba stared shamelessly. "Now I see. Now I know how to see. I beg your pardon most humbly, but what is your name?"

"Zosia," the most beautiful waitress in the world replied with dignity. "Zosia, vintage 1939."

"We're very pleased to meet you, Miss Zosia, vintage 1939," Mr.

Trąba bowed, "very pleased to meet you. We are unknown partisans from Wisła."

"Partisans don't eat pastry," Zosia vintage 1939 burst out laughing.

"Oh, Miss Zosia, you've obviously had very little to do with partisans in your life. And what does your esteemed boyfriend do?"

"He plays soccer for Legia," she said without enthusiasm, and she added after a moment, "but he isn't my boyfriend. I don't love him. I beg the gentlemen partisans' pardon, but the chef is calling me."

And indeed, in the open doors, gleaming with golden radiance like the Gates of Heaven and leading to the kitchen and back rooms, there appeared an incredible cook in an incredible cap, and Zosia vintage 1939 turned on her heel and, like a gazelle, ran in his direction.

"Indeed, the star of the beauty standing on the curb on Wiślna Street is beginning to fade," said Mr. Trąba, casting nostalgic glances. "But you have to admit, Chief, a white blouse and a black skirt are the absolute peak of perfection in a woman's wardrobe. Never, nowhere, can any woman put on a more perfect vestment than a white blouse and a black skirt. That's right. A white blouse and a black skirt. Accessories worthy of the deepest analysis. We will have something to debate on the return trip. But now," Mr. Trąba drank a sip of lemon squash and sat more comfortably in his chair, "but now, gentlemen, you will permit me to occupy your attention with more fundamental questions."

·

"When you, Chief, announced that traveling relaxes you, I also realized that I felt some relief on account of leaving, even for a short while, the Cieszyn region, that chosen land of home-grown philosophers. But in addition to relief, fear began to well up in my heart, uncertainty, and a horrible craving for you know what. I thought to myself: the thing we are attempting is contradictory to our natures to such an extent that there is no way that it could succeed, because it won't succeed. The demon of capitulation made itself at home in my heart. For our drama, Chief, is based upon the fact that, by reason of birth, upbringing, confession, nature, and psychophysical predisposition, we are unquestionably not assassins. We are rather, for all the above-mentioned reasons, and a thousand other causes, born negotiators. After all, in the depths of my soul I would rather negotiate with him than kill him. Instead of initiating and, what is worse, definitively embodying my grand plan in the face of death, I would rather, I would rather a hundred times over, that we go to that Gomułka of theirs and say: 'It's like this and like that, comrade, in a word, it would be better if you went away, it would be better if you went away, you Polish Genghis Khan.' We could even dazzle him with an ambiguous compliment, drink a glass with him, and take care of the whole matter amicably."

"Our cause has utterly failed, Comrade Secretary. You are going away, we remain," said Father.

Mr. Trąba was so delighted that he snorted, choked on his own saliva, and got up from his place.

"A masterpiece, simply a masterpiece. I have to say, you rarely speak up, but when you do, it's a masterpiece."

"As usual, I was quoting *The People's Tribune*," Father smiled gloomily.

"The good use of a quotation is often worth more than an original thought, but the use of any quotation from *The People's Tribune*—in such a way that it *makes sense*—heightens its sense and makes it an original thought . . . One way or the other, those are fantasies," Mr. Trąba continued after a moment of silence, "one way or the other. Perhaps we are born negotiators, but we assassins *in spe* are also just plain good and gentle people. And even if we were to reach him, and even if we were to explain our reasons to him—we are staying, you are going away, and so on—well, he would begin to drown us in his ironsmith-Leninist logorrhea. He would begin to convince us. Mrs. Gomułka would extract a bottle of French cognac from the sideboard and serve us home-baked cake . . . That's right, Chief, she cooks and bakes at home. In this sense, our emperor lives modestly.

"There are testimonies of the members of the Central Committee who, in 1956, visited Gomułka at home for the purpose of transferring power over this country to him. So this was the scene: the coronation ceremony was going on in the dining room, and an unceasing and horrible racket in the kitchen kept interrupting them. It was Mrs. Gomułka pounding pork cutlets on the cutting board . . . And at this point the aura of domesticity would doubtless seduce us too. From word to word, slowly, slowly, we would begin to nod our approval.

From up close, the tyrant would begin to seem less and less deadly, less and less bloody, and in the end, convinced and defeated, we would go away with nothing, while he would remain, and, what is more, he would be strengthened in his power. There's nothing to be done for it," Mr. Trąba sighed, "nothing to be done for it. We have to kill him."

Mr. Trąba lifted yet another cream pastry to his mouth, ate it slowly, exquisite bite after exquisite bite, drank a sip of coffee, drank a sip of lemon squash, and spoke further:

"I have no choice. Since I don't know how to do anything, I can't choose the field in which I could accomplish something before dying. I can't dance, I can't drive a car, I can't ski, I can't swim, I don't speak languages, I haven't mastered the axe or any other tool, I don't know about nature, nor am I a technician, or a humanist. I don't know about art or literature, I'm not a tinker or a collector, I'm not even, contrary to appearances, a flirt who flirts by listing his insufficiencies. My pal from the school bench, the most reverend bishop, stuck it out, finished, defended, wrote, worked, conducted activities, directed parishes, climbed up the rungs until he became a bishop of the Church. I don't envy him, although of course every time I think of him I also think that if my life hadn't been a disastrous life, but an edifying one, that his life would have been my life. Although that isn't true either— that I don't envy him. I *do* envy him. I envy him horribly, that he can send postcards to Mrs. Chief from every corner of the world, and I envy the care with which your spouse, Chief, collects, preserves, and orders that casual correspondence . . .

"Of course there were moments in my wasted life when I got the audacious idea in my head to gain mastery of some earthly skill other than drinking, but upon reflection I rejected all those ideas. I drank all my life, and drinking was my work and my rest, my love and my hobby. Drinking was my art, my concert, and my artfully written sonnet. Drinking was my cognition, my description, my synthesis, and my analysis. Only amateurs, laymen, and graphomaniacs assert that you drink in order to soften the monstrosity of the world and to dull unbearable sensitivity. On the contrary, you drink in order to deepen pain and to heighten sensitivity. Especially in a case like mine: when there is nothing but drinking, it is necessary to make an art of drinking, it is necessary to reach the heart of the matter through drinking, and the heart of the matter is death. Since man is condemned to pain, since man condemns himself to pain, it is necessary to become a virtuoso of pain. And I, Józef Trąba, Grand Master of my own pain, now, when my bodily shell refuses to execute the only ability it possessed, I, Józef Trąba, have resolved that, before I die on account of one of seven unfailing reasons, I have resolved to take possession of one more, a one-time earthly ability, and that is, as we have known for a long time, the ability to kill First Secretary Władysław Gomułka.

"And so that there be absolute clarity," Mr. Trąba raised his voice slightly, "so that there be absolute clarity, I wish to emphasize with all force that I do not blame Moscow for my unhappy fate. You, Chief, you were debased by Moscow, me—no way. No one bears the blame for my fate other than myself. If I were a truly great personality, I would cope with everything. Moscow, I grant you, is tearing this country apart, frustrating every initiative, befouling and debasing people, but truly great personalities can cope with Moscow. After all, strictly speaking, you can't even say that Moscow poses a genuine challenge for truly great personalities, because it doesn't pose one, it isn't any partner, it isn't any opponent, you can basically cope with it with childish ease. In spite of Moscow, a truly great personality will learn foreign languages, study the classics, plumb the depths of philosophy, listen to the great composers, even travel. A truly great personality will cope with the velvet Russification of this country by gaining perfect mastery of the language of Gogol, because, after all, that isn't the language of Stalin. That's right, Chief, if I were just a tiny bit stronger person, I would have sovereign mastery over myself and my innumerable abilities. But since it is entirely otherwise, I enter into history by the narrow path of the barbarian."

Mr. Trąba glanced at his watch, then he cast his gaze over us and the dark interior of the confectioner's shop, as if he were seeking the willowy shadow of the most beautiful waitress in the world, and he said:

"Time to pay the bill and do our duty."

•

We stood in the penetrating cold, under leafless poplars. The rain had stopped. November constellations revolved above us.

"It won't be long now," Mr. Trąba said, and with a delicate motion he removed the crossbow from my shoulders. "After they return, the guards draw the shutters over the windows on the ground floor, so that no one can see how they swill vodka and play cards. But in his apartment on the second floor, the shutters, sometimes even the curtains, are left open until late at night. Accidental passersby and neighbors say that you can often see him quite well, especially when he stands in the window and smokes a cigarette, half a cigarette, since, for reasons of economy, he smokes halves. In glass cigarette holders."

"Are you certain you will hit him? Do you even know how to shoot that thing?" I had the impression that, for the first time since the beginning of the expedition, Father had taken an interest in the real course of events, and that for the first time he had taken a look at the Chinese crossbow and arrow.

"I know how, and I will hit him," Mr. Trąba replied, and his whisper was icy.

"Just exactly where and when did you learn and practice?" Father continued his inquiry.

"Chief! And do you believe in God? You do believe, don't you? And how did you arrive at proficiency and skill in faith? You didn't scheme. You didn't wrestle with the problem of whether or not the grace of faith had been granted to you. You simply went to Sunday school, to lessons in religion, to confirmation class. You recited prayers, you sang Psalms—in a word, you behaved in general and in every regard like a pure-bred, believing, full-blooded Protestant, and before you knew it you *were* a pure-bred, believing, full-blooded Protestant . . . You see, it's just the same with shooting a crossbow."

"You'll forgive me, but your reasoning is a bit difficult for me to follow, Mr. Trąba."

"I'm concerned with the spiritual aspect," Mr. Trąba started to giggle unexpectedly and in a very peculiar manner. "I'm concerned with the spiritual aspect, plus practice, of course. Training is the way of life. Moreover, one mustn't forget that this," Mr. Trąba raised the crossbow to his shoulder, "is the weapon of the ancient Chinese. Therefore, one must take into account the teachings of the ancient Chinese. And the ancient Chinese say that when you shoot at your target, you must free yourself from trivial thoughts of the necessity of hitting it. The shot must have a spiritual scope, whereas the shooter must remain in intense tension until the shot falls upon the target like a ripe fruit falling, like snow from a bamboo leaf . . ."

You could hear approaching cars and motorcycles, the slamming of doors. Lights were lit in the dark windows at which we had been staring for a good hour. Mr. Trąba extracted the arrow with the silver tip from the tails of his raincoat—it had been secured there on special loops that Mother had sewn on the coat—and, with unusual solicitude, he placed it on the bed of the crossbow. Terrifying cawing resounded. There must have been a thousand funereal birds sitting in the bushes.

"Crows live several hundred years. They will remember this moment centuries after our deaths," said Father.

"Not only they," Mr. Trąba took careful aim in the direction of the illuminated windows, "not only they will remember, Chief . . . There he is! I see him! The ancient Chinese teach us to bow to the target before hitting it."

Mr. Trąba tore the crossbow off his shoulder for a moment, bowed, placed it back in a flash, and, almost without aiming, drew the trigger. I heard the whistle of the arrow, the shattering of the windowpane. An absolute quiet ensued; even the crows fell silent. After a moment, a woman's desperate cry resounded, a dog began to bark, we heard footsteps, someone was running in our direction.

"Got him. Let's split up," Mr. Trąba spoke with an incredibly calm, almost sleepy voice. Jerzyk will run to his woman friend. We, Chief, will head in the direction of the station, but by different paths. To the glory of the Fatherland, gentlemen." Mr. Trąba reached back broadly and fluidly and hurled the crossbow into the crown of the tree. The crows took flight. The Chinese crossbow hung in the invisible heights.

·

I ran through the dark little streets, and I swallowed tears. I don't know why. Maybe I was sorry to lose the crossbow that had burdened me so unbearably all day. I was sorry to lose the irrevocably lost toy, and even today, whenever I am in Warsaw, whenever I am in this wolfish city, which is now like a Biblical emporium, every time, I stand under that poplar and, with head thrown back, strain to catch sight of the shape of a Chinese crossbow that has become one for all eternity with the branches and boughs, has been covered over by generations of leaves. I ran through the little streets, and I fell into the dark gate, and I climbed the dark stairs, and the angel of my first love, not changed in the least, in that same mid-thigh sweater, opened the door to me, and, just as I had supposed, she showed no sign of surprise upon seeing me. And the entire evening I sat at the table, and I played chess with her husband. She changed dresses in the depths of the apartment, combed her hair before a mirror, and gave me secret and tender signs from time to time. And so I played with him, and I waited for the moment—the moment that the gestures of her incredible fingers had foretold—to arrive. I waited until, sooner or later, he would fall asleep over the chessboard, but he didn't show any signs of falling asleep. He meditated for hours over the simplest move. It was rather I who was falling off to sleep, and in the first half-sleep I heard her delicate steps. She walked up to the television. A cadaverous light fell over the chessboard. Then serious music resounded, and an announcer in an incredible jacket pronounced the words that I had long known would be pronounced in every home that evening. He pronounced the word "death," and the word "attempt," and the word "assassination." And then there appeared on the screen skyscrapers and automobiles of a sort I had never seen on the road, and yet on the blurry close-up you could see how the President of the United States, John Fitzgerald Kennedy, sitting in the open limousine, grabbed his pierced neck, how someone jumped to his rescue, but there wasn't any possibility of rescue, for the shot was on target and unerring, like snow falling from a bamboo leaf.

Very late in the night, the angel of my first love came to me. She sat on the edge of the bed and held my hand. On the other side of the wall snored her unhappy husband, who, granted, had beaten me at chess, but whom she had never loved. My first dream began, and through its first spaces, over snow-capped mountains, flew an arrow with a silver tip. It circled the world like a Russky sputnik, and the slashed air immediately sealed over it, and there wasn't a trace of its passing.

Chapter IX

I BREATHED IN DEEPLY, AND UNEXPECTEDLY I CAUGHT THE SMELL
of freshly mown grass. Perhaps the desert thread of a tropical atmospheric front had slipped over the icy valley. Or perhaps the clear well
of a thaw was slowly opening up among the dark, murky heavens.

"Jesus Christ is born," said Mr. Trąba. He reeled and leaned on my
shoulder. "Jesus Christ is born, and although this happens every year,
and although He is born every year, although every year Reverend
Father Pastor Potraffke tells of this in sermons that become more and
more formally perfect, you can never get to the bottom of this story
or investigate it completely . . ."

You could hear the far-off drone of an engine. In a gray cloud
stirred up by tires, a truck loaded with bushy spruce trees drove down
from Buffalo Mountain.

"That's a fine thing," Mr. Trąba grumbled, glancing at his watch.
"It's already almost 10:00, it's 9:47 to be precise. In two hours Sexton
Messerschmidt, and with him all the bell-ringers in all the basilicas in
the world, will pull on the ropes, organists will strike their keyboards,
songs praising the advent of the Lord will reverberate, and these lag-
gards are still cutting down a stand of trees."

And Mr. Trąba, realizing his own tardiness, shakily hastened his step. It wasn't far now. We passed by the Baptists, who were already plunged in darkness, and Rychter Department Store buzzed with the flames of huge candles and the hubbub of conversations. For a moment, a cyclone of snow, smelling of gasoline, embraced us. In its eye a lost truck swam slowly. A huge dog ran after it like a specter and barked like mad. It seemed to me that, above its barking and above the Latin carols sung by shepherds and angels, I heard the stormy signal of Radio Free Europe. It was ten o'clock, and every day, Christmas Eve or not, without fail, with desperate vengeance in his eyes, Father turned the radio up full blast.

Indeed, you could never get to the bottom of that story, nor investigate it completely. Every year the mixed forests on Buffalo Mountain froze. Every year Caesar Augustus called for all the world to be taxed. Every year Mr. Trąba was late for Christmas Eve.

.

Mother was covering the table with a cloth. In the middle she put salt, garlic, and communion wafers. She placed a candle stick and a tea cup with honey. The smell of milk, fish, and cabbage came from the kitchen. I brought hymnals and set them out at the places on the table. I knew the hymns by heart. I knew "Time of Joy," number 139 in the hymnal of Father Heczko, and "Praise Be to Thee, Jesus Christ," number 127, and all twelve verses of "From Heaven High I Come to You." Everybody—Father, Mother, Mr. Trąba, Elżunia Baptystka, and Grand Master Swaczyna—everybody in our parts, even Małgosia Snyperek, even Commandant Jeremiah, everybody knew the hymns by heart, although they glanced at the hymnals while singing, as if renewing a covenant with the old books. They glanced at the words of the hymns, even though they didn't read them. It was rather that, by singing, they brought them to life, praised them through their singing, strengthened the fading print by singing, and reinforced the crumbling pages by singing. Everybody knew the hymns by heart, but I don't think anyone but me knew all twelve verses of "From Heaven High I Come to You." No one but me—and Father Pastor Potraffke. Even today I am still ready to recite or sing that entire festive hymn, and—no doubt when I say this I am consumed by Evangelical-Augsburg pride—I am ready to say or even to sing all twelve verses, and verily I say unto you, I will do it just as well as, more than thirty years ago, Father Pastor Potraffke did it in the Protestant Hall.

·

"From heaven high I come to you,
I bring you tidings good and new;
Glad tidings of great joy I bring,
Whereof I now will say and sing:
To you this night is born a child,
Of Mary, chosen virgin mild;
This little child, of lowly birth,
Shall be the joy of all the earth."

Pastor Potraffke stood against the backdrop of a plush curtain that covered the stage of the Protestant Hall. He descended from the heavens and sang. The Pastor's Wife, beautiful and dark-complexioned like the Brazilian actress Maria Félix, leaned lower and lower over the keyboard. Snow was falling beyond the high windows. The church tower rose beyond the moveable wall of snow.

"To you this night is born a child,
Of Mary, chosen virgin mild . . ."

Father Pastor Potraffke finally stood on the lowest level of the ladder with fireworks shooting from every step. He touched the earth with his foot, and he suddenly fell silent, as if struck by a subterranean thunderbolt that came from the depths of the globe, from the basement of the Protestant Hall. The Pastor's Wife played a moment longer, glanced once, twice in the direction of her husband, played a few chords more loudly and distinctly, as if wishing to persuade him to sing further, glanced once again with reflection and attention, and her divine shoulders, covered with a cashmere shawl, shook, her fragile fingers tore themselves suddenly from the keyboard, a blush covered her indescribable face.

"A child is born to you this night!" Pastor Potraffke suddenly bellowed. "Heathens! A child is born to you this night!" Apoplectic patches appeared on his chubby-cheeked face, and his eyes burned with an apostolic radiance. "Sons of philistines," he shrieked at the boys sitting at the window, "sons of philistines! A child is born to you this night! And you," in a fury he turned his face to the girls sitting by the door, "and you, daughters . . ." he hesitated for a moment, "and you, daughters of Bolsheviks! A child is born to you this night!" he finished as if with a sort of relief. "Nothing in the world," he wheezed, drowning in the ocean of his own impotence, "nothing, verily I say unto you, nothing will bring me to grant you confirmation. For the next time, that will be after the holidays, for the next time, six verses, not six, *seven* verses, by heart, of 'From Heaven High I Come to You,' seven verses of that festive hymn, which . . . who composed it? Well, who?" Potraffke looked around the Protestant Hall with what seemed a more conscious glance. "Błaszczyk, let Błaszczyk tell us: who composed the festive hymn 'From Heaven High I Come to You?'"

Straw-haired Joey stood up uncertainly, glanced at the thicker and thicker snow beyond the windows, at the white cross on the wall, at the Pastor's Wife, who, with an exquisite motion of her head, was indicating the portrait of Martin Luther hanging on the wall, and at father Pastor Potraffke, who was blocking his view of that portrait, and he said, not quite asking, not quite answering:

"Father Pastor?"

"No, not me, you mutton-brain." The furies left Pastor Potraffke, and he spoke with an almost normal, only slightly stifled, voice. "No, not me, mutton-head. It was our Reformer, Doctor Martin Luther. Yes, verily I say unto you, our Reformer, Doctor Martin Luther, composed that hymn on Christmas Eve in the year of our Lord 1534 in his home in Wittenberg. Sit down, Błaszczyk. I understand that the Lord receives various people at His table, but every time I look at you, Błaszczyk, I wonder. Verily, I say unto you, Błaszczyk," Pastor Potraffke again raised his voice, "verily, I say unto you, Błaszczyk, I wonder whether someone like you can sit down to the Lord's table."

The Pastor's Wife suddenly struck the keyboard, and we all eagerly sang the hymn which ended the lessons and services:

"Amen, Amen, Amen,
Jesus Christ is Lord . . ."

We quickly recited the prayer, and we set off for houses that smelled of apples, poppyseed strudels, and floor polish.

Dressed in his old postal uniform, Father chopped huge beach logs in the courtyard.

"And what did you learn today?" he asked with a skepticism that was rare with him and, paradoxically, foretold a good mood.

"Nothing yet. I am only now going to go learn it. The pastor told us to learn seven verses of 'From Heaven High I Come to You' by heart. For the holidays," I added with emphasis and hope.

For it now and then happened that Father, adhering to all of the principles formulated in Scripture, and subject, at the same time, to uncontrollable fancies, came to the conclusion that a contradiction had arisen between the commandments of the Bible and my homework assignments, and he would forbid me from doing them. "You aren't going to solve any equations on Sunday," he would say now and then. "You must keep the Sabbath holy."

But this time it was different.

"Seven verses of 'From Heaven High I Come to You.'" He struck with precision in just the right place, and the beach trunk was split asunder, revealing its almost brick-red interior against the background of the all-encompassing snow. "If I were you," he said with his characteristic, non-binding tone, "if I were you, I'd learn all twelve verses. A person ought to strive for perfection. 'Be ye therefore perfect, even as your Father which is in heaven is perfect.'"

•

I placed the hymnals on the table cloth with numbing symmetry. "Be ye perfect, even as the hand that places you is perfect," I whispered. Mother sliced the bread that Mrs. Wantuła had baked in Goje. She sliced for a long time and attentively, and when she had finished, she first glanced at the table, then at Father, and she said with an indulgence that turned inexorably in the course of speaking into impatience:

"We're missing apples, nuts, and Mr. Trąba."

Then she went up to the window, moved the yellow curtain aside, and stared for a long time into the windy labyrinths of the Christmas Eve night, which was thickening from the constantly falling snow.

"The Baptists went to bed long ago. The lights are turned out, but we haven't even sat down at the table yet," she said, tearing her forehead away from the dark-blue windowpane.

Father, dressed in a white shirt, smelling of cognac and still inflamed from the afternoon fish-slaughter, stood by the table, took coins and banknotes from his wallet, and slid them under the tablecloth. The heretical habits of the Baptists didn't make much of an impression, either on him or on us.

"The poor things," was all mother would say from time to time, "the poor things! What will those poor things say at the Lord's Judgment?"

"They won't say anything. They will say that they had gotten lost, and that will be that. The Lord God forgives those who've gotten lost," Małgosia Snyperek would respond every time over her cup of coffee, which she took "Turkish" style.

Especially when the Christmas holidays came, the Baptists gave the impression of being completely lost in their heterodox misfortune. They would sit down to their Christmas Eve meals at some Godlessly early hour, when it was still light. They didn't share communion hosts, they didn't give each other presents, they didn't eat fish. True, they did have cabbage and white roll with milk among their Christmas Eve dishes, they hung apples and candy on the tree, but all of that was too little. The untimely slumber of the Baptists was too weak an argument to incline Father to put a sheepskin coat over his shoulders and set off to find Mr. Trąba, who was undoubtedly dawdling over wrapping his presents.

Only when Mother placed the tray with immaculately sliced bread on the table, when next to it she set homemade butter in a wooden butter-dish, when she placed apples on the piano, when she set crystal dishes with nuts and rum-flavored crescent rolls next to them, only then, when she took off the light-blue cretonne apron and began to fold it with slow and alarmingly precise motions, only then would Father raise his hand, with a gesture that was neither calming nor indicating an announcement, and say with preacherly passion:

"I know, I know, I know. The Catholics will be going to midnight Mass any minute now, and we still haven't sat down to our Christmas Eve supper."

And he would put on his sheepskin coat and hat and set off in a hurry to find Mr. Trąba, whom he would usually meet somewhere nearby anyway, often right next to the Rychter Department Store, or even closer. And so, most often they both would reappear much more quickly than we expected. Sometimes it would seem like a demonstration from a private conjuror's séance. Father would stand in the doorway, go out, the doors would shut, the doors would open, and in that same moment they both would already be standing on the threshold, Father and Mr. Trąba, awaited for so many hours now already, and yet it was as if he had suddenly materialized out of thin air. And immediately Mr. Trąba would begin to explain himself, to apologize for being late. Presents awkwardly wrapped in gray packing paper and tied with faded ribbons would pour from under his coat. He would hand them to us right there in the hall, as if flummoxed by his own awkwardness and uncertain whether, on account of that awkwardness, the presents would last to the end of the supper.

"You will forgive me, Mrs. Chief," he would say to Mother, "but according to our carol," Mr. Trąba didn't quite speak, didn't quite sing, "'Give Lord God a joyous evening, joyous night, first for the lord.' So here for you, Chief, instead of the proverbial Christmas Eve brandy I bring paschal slivovitz, *ergo* paschal Christmas Eve brandy. And what would you say about a drink stamped with such an eschatological oxymoron? Paschal Christmas Eve brandy! What would you say? 'Give, Lord God, a joyous evening, joyous night, first for the lord, then also for such a lady.' Mrs. Chief, please be so kind as to accept this small expression of homage from a suffering admirer, who, the more often he sees you—you will forgive me, Chief, but the late Sigmund Freud taught you, too, that the suppression of the life of the impulses turns against you—and so, Mrs. Chief, a small expression of homage from an admirer who suffers tortures, such that, the more he sees you, the greater the tortures he suffers."

And Mr. Trąba handed Mother the neatest little package, and she delicately undid the little ribbon and half-opened the paper, and with a girlishly lit-up face she examined a tiny little bottle of "Chat noir" perfume and a dark green silk scarf that suited her perfectly.

"'Give, Lord God, a joyous evening, joyous night,'" now Mr. Trąba was singing with full voice, "'First for the lord, then also for such a lady. And for his dearest servants. And for his dearest servants.'"

And Mr. Trąba would turn to me, and invariably he handed me a book.

"This, Jerzyk, is currently the most widely read book in People's Poland: *The Ugly Duchess* by Lion Feuchtwanger. As literature, it is rather mediocre stuff and every bit the popular sort, but of course we ought to proclaim eternal glory to Comrade Gomułka for expressing his consent to the publishing of a novel that was, without a doubt, absolutely unintelligible to him. As I say, Jerzyk, this is not great writing, but when on the first and second days of Christmas you sit down, well stocked with nuts and sweets, next to the well-lit furnace, you will have this appropriate, relaxing, and even, in some minimal degree, edifying reading."

"Between the city of Innsbruck and the monastery of Wilten a large open piece of level ground was covered with tents and flagpoles," I read the first sentence of *The Ugly Duchess*. Father stared at the Hebrew alphabet on the violet-golden book jacket.

"Sit down, sit down, sit down," Mother always called out three times as she hurried to the kitchen.

.

But this time, as soon as Father began, with desperate passion, to speak his threefold "I know, I know, I know," Mother—already after his first "I know"—said, "Sit," and with classically feminine thoughtlessness, she destroyed the entire finely-wrought construction of mythical repetition.

"Sit," she said. "Have you already forgotten what happened last year? He'll go," and she looked at me. "Put on your hat, coat, and gloves, and go get Mr. Trąba. You know where Daddy's Siamese brother lives? Beyond the Protestant Hall on the left."

The humiliating supposition that I might not know where Mr. Trąba lived didn't even particularly sting me. It was probably the first time that I had stood in for Father in a crucial matter, and I put on my hat, coat, and gloves, trying to lend an unhurried male decisiveness to my gestures. In fact, last year Father had gone out for Mr. Trąba, and, after a good hour, Mother whispered with whitened lips, "They have both disappeared for all eternity." And when after an eternity they finally appeared, they were drunk as lords, joyous, and inordinately roused intellectually.

"All the best, Chief," Mr. Trąba leaned over the table like Pastor Potraffke over the edge of the pulpit. "Lord Jesus has already begun His reign, Chief, although this is still hidden from the eyes of Comrade First Secretary Władysław Gomułka, just as in days of old it was hidden from the eyes of Caesar Augustus. But both of them, both of them, Chief, both Caesar Augustus and Secretary Gomułka already serve Lord Jesus. It was said by the prophets that the Savior would be born in Bethlehem. And whose doing was it that the Holy Family found itself in Bethlehem? It was the doing of Caesar Augustus, who gave out the decree, for if he hadn't given out the decree, Joseph and Mary would certainly have remained in Nazareth. And just as the great Caesar Augustus had to serve Christ with his decree, contributing to the fact that His birth happened in Bethlehem in accordance with the prophecies, so also First Secretary Władysław Gomułka has to serve Christ by raising the price of boneless beef, contributing in this very way to the fact that, in accordance with what was said by the prophets, Communism will fall . . . All the best, Chief."

The communion wafer, dipped in honey, shook dangerously in Mr. Trąba's restless fingers. Mother looked at the drop that was falling onto the table cloth as if she wished to cut off its flight with some desperate motion, or perhaps to turn back the course of events the prophets had foretold.

·

I breathed in deeply. The snow had unexpectedly stopped falling, and in the sudden motionlessness you could hear the regular blows of the axes that came from the forests on Buffalo Mountain. Someone was laughing there with an unbridled pagan laugh. Someone wastefully started and stopped an engine. In the depths of the perspective that was brightening like the Milky Way, beyond the Rychter Department Store, beyond the Baptists plunged in darkness, loomed Mr. Trąba's silhouette, ambling with its characteristic wobbliness.

The Rychters were sitting around an oval table in the dining room on the ground floor. In the corner, a Christmas tree as large as a royal sailing-ship burned with a thousand candles. Through the high, unveiled windows I saw the incredible figure of Mrs. Rychter gliding in from the kitchen. She carried a tureen full of *barszcz* or mushroom soup raised up in her athletic arms.

"Merry Christmas, Jerzyk," said Mr. Trąba. "To tell you the truth, after last year's excesses, I was expecting that you and not the Chief would come out to meet me. But 'Give Lord God a joyous evening, joyous night'—what sort of excesses were they anyway? In the end we made it to matins, if memory doesn't fail me. And if it is about the excessive theological freedom that takes possession of me in such situations, I can't do anything about it. I am, Jerzyk, a truly lonely person, and all forms of the presence of God make *special*, sometimes downright troublesomely *inspiring*, impressions on truly lonely people."

The gate leading to the Rychter Department Store suddenly opened. The bulky figure of Mrs. Rychter appeared. Her arms were still raised up. At first, I thought that she was still holding up the steaming— no, no longer steaming, but now also flaming—tureen of *barszcz* or mushroom soup. A gigantic flame, in the shape of a conifer, blazed from the tureen. The beautiful Christmas tree, majestic like a royal sailing-ship, burned over Mrs. Rychter's head. You could hear the closer and closer barking of a St. Bernard, huge like a specter, returning from a futile chase. The greedy roar of the fire. Ornaments were bursting. The angel hair was sizzling. Mrs. Rychter ran with heavy leaps through the deep snow, like a bemedalled record holder who is supposed to carry the sacred flame to the Olympic arena. She made two, or maybe three circles, stopped over a great pile of snow, and, holding the gigantic torch with both hands, she began to beat the ground with it furiously, rhythmically, as if she wished to flog the disobedient elements with the fire and the glass.

"Mrs. Rychter, whatever are you doing? After all, you're supposed to put snow on the Lord's tree, and not the other way around—not the Lord's tree into the snow!" Mr. Trąba called out with the greatest amazement. "It's a waste of prewar and post-German Christmas tree decorations. It's even a waste of Bolshevik adornments . . ."

But Mrs. Rychter, as if afraid a gigantic worldwide conflagration would start from her Christmas tree, beat the snowy dune frenziedly. The snow glistened. Shreds of ornamental piping and remnants of bulbs flew up into the air, as if in praise of the Lord. Soon it had all gone out, and, still holding the grimy stump in both hands (the remaining mast of the burned sailing-ship), Mrs. Rychter wordlessly disappeared behind the gate to the department store.

"Women." Mr. Trąba waived his hand with an omniscient gesture.

The dog, huge like a specter, made smaller and smaller circles around us, barked venomously, wheezed with the choked hoarse voice of the predator readying himself to jump. Almost reflexively, I picked up a lump of frozen snow.

"Don't you even dare, Jerzy," Mr. Trąba said gently, "don't you even dare. It's never right to raise your hand against one of God's creatures, but especially not on a night like tonight."

And Mr. Trąba whistled knowingly and amicably patted his knee, and the monster that was coming closer and closer, made furious by our nonchalance, wheezed hatefully and flashed his yellowish fangs, and his entrails, accustomed to digesting human flesh, gave out a piercing whine. He was a bit reminiscent of Bryś the Man-Eater, who belonged to Commandant Jeremiah, but, paralyzed by my fear, I wasn't entirely certain of it.

"You never know what sort of spirit rattles around in the bowels of beasts." Mr. Trąba seemed to pay absolutely no attention to Bryś the Man-Eater, or his twin brother from hell, who was cutting off every possible road of return and flight. "Jesus Christ is born, Jerzyk, and although He is born this year for the one thousand nine hundred and sixty-third time, He has come, up to now, only one time, and He will come once more. The first time, Jerzyk. And the second time, Jerzyk. But we don't know when that second time will be, nor do even the angels know. It is said that the second time He will come in glory and on clouds, but who knows, who knows what the order of things will be? Perhaps He will first appear in invisibility and reticence, and will clothe Himself in glory only after that. The first time He came,

He appeared in human form and not even in that of an angel. And yet, after all, Jerzyk, angels are more glorious creatures than are we, but nonetheless merciful God honored us more and lowered Himself more to us than to the angels, when, on that night, He became a man and not an angel. Who knows, Jerzyk, whether at His second coming He won't lower Himself even further in His infinite humility, who knows whether He won't come as an even less glorious creature, who knows whether He won't appear first in the shape of a panther or a she-wolf, and only then, once he casts the beastly covering from Himself, will He judge us in the golden clouds of glory . . ."

We were already standing by the house, but the man-eating dog had also drawn nearer—at a distance of one decisive leap.

"Bryś, Bryś," Mr. Trąba said gently. And the man-eater crouched. His eyes glistened cadaverously. He lurked for yet another second, before the final leap in the direction of our throats.

And then Mr. Trąba raised up his hand, just as Pastor Potraffke sometimes raised his in the pulpit, just as Father would raise his before he said his threefold "I know, I know, I know;" and then Mr. Trąba raised up his hand, just as the Savior raised up His to calm the agitated waves, and with his hand raised, Mr. Trąba said distinctly:

"Brysław, verily I say unto Thee, Brysław: come unto me!"

And as if amused by the incredible buffoonery of this whole scene, the dog suddenly wagged its tail as a sign of peace, jumped on its front paws, now to the one side, now to the other, and at a little trot he approached us and began to fawn at our feet. Mr. Trąba produced a communion wafer from his breast pocket and stuck it into the muzzle that had been miraculously transformed into Good itself. And the dog, delicately taking the Christmas Eve missive between its fangs, began to withdraw. He made greater and greater circles. It looked as if he were running off to share the communion wafer Mr. Trąba had offered him with other creatures, or perhaps to tell them the glad tidings of creation.

We went up the stairs, shook the snow off our shoes. A key turned in the lock. Father opened the door for us.

143

Jerzy Pilch is one of Poland's most important contemporary writers and journalists—Czesław Miłosz once called him "the hope of young Polish prose." In addition to his long-running satirical newspaper column, Pilch has published several novels, and he has been nominated for Poland's prestigious NIKE Literary Award four times; he won the award in 2001 for *The Mighty Angel*, also available from Open Letter.

David Frick is a Professor in the Department of Slavic Languages and Literatures at the University of California, Berkeley.

Open Letter—the University of Rochester's nonprofit, literary translation press—is one of only a handful of publishing houses dedicated to increasing access to world literature for English readers. Publishing ten titles in translation each year, Open Letter searches for works that are extraordinary and influential, works that we hope will become the classics of tomorrow.

Making world literature available in English is crucial to opening our cultural borders, and its availability plays a vital role in maintaining a healthy and vibrant book culture. Open Letter strives to cultivate an audience for these works by helping readers discover imaginative, stunning works of fiction and by creating a constellation of international writing that is engaging, stimulating, and enduring.

Current and forthcoming titles from Open Letter include works from France, Germany, Iceland, Russia, South Africa, and numerous other countries.

www.openletterbooks.org